HONOR STUDENT

By Michael Russell

Honor Student

Once Upon a Time on a Bicycle

Winterdanse: The Misplaced Art of Snow Ballet

The Unfounding of America: A Countdown to Too Late

Forthcoming

Little Girl, Big Lie

Knights of the Eleventh Hour

The Inquisition of Don Miguel

Also from Nonesmanneslond

Paw to Pointe: An Irrefutable Coalition of
Canine Wisdom and Ballet Truth

by Sallyann Mulcahy

H·O·N·O·R STUDENT

Michael Russell

HONOR STUDENT
Copyright © 1989, 2019 by Michael Russell

nonesmanneslond.com

Nonesmanneslond
32.7089649°N, -108.5381073°W

Russell, Michael, 1957 -
Honor Student

ISBN 978-0-9998730-3-8
Trade Paperback
vi

Honor Student is available in hardcover and
trade-paperback bindings. Editions Nonesmanneslond
publishes ink-on-paper books exclusively.

SECOND EDITION

To anyone who has ever attended public school,
but particularly to those whose minds
may yet survive it.

MENCKEN

The most erroneous assumption is to the effect that the aim of public education is to fill the young of the species with knowledge and awaken their intelligence, and so make them fit to discharge the duties of citizenship in an enlightened and independent manner. Nothing could be further from the truth.

The aim of public education is not to spread enlightenment at all; it is simply to reduce as many individuals as possible to the same safe level, to breed and train a standardized citizenry, to put down dissent and originality. That is its aim in the United States, whatever the pretensions of politicians, pedagogues, and other such mountebanks, and that is its aim everywhere else.

H.L. Mencken, 1880-1956
. . . *The American Mercury*

CONTENTS

PREFACE

Honor Student, 1989

I began making notes for the first edition of *Honor Student* during the winter of 1982, four years prior to typing the manuscript's opening line. While unwrapping the lunch I had packed for my first day as a substitute English teacher at a New Hampshire high school, I found myself dumbstruck by the immature empty conversations surrounding me. It had been seven years since I was last in a room full of chatting teenagers, but there was not a teenager in sight. This was the teacher's lounge.

A dozen or so women and men were seated around tables or standing beside a counter with a sink, coffee service, and water dispenser. Except for the lack of bell bottoms and polyester, they were dressed like my high-school teachers. Except for the diminished age difference between us, they could have been my high-school teachers.

Except, I was certain, *my* teachers would never have sounded so average, so unteacher-like, when conversing beyond earshot of their students. Would they?

I spent half of that period hoping to hear something that would inspire me to entrust the education of children to these particular educators, then returned disappointed to my empty classroom to finish my lunch.

What, I wondered, had I expected?

I was at the time passionately immersed in a career I had chosen from among three contenders, one of which had been teaching high-school English. My path, like that of many professional athletes, was competitive, self-driven, and uncompromising, and although the standards I set as an athlete permeated every aspect of my life, I realized they were not necessarily the standards of others, and that I should not expect them to be.

But this was *education*.

This place was where parents sent their children to learn what was needed for *life*. This place was where professional educators ministered a responsibility only marginally less important than parenting and considerably more important than doctoring.

This place was sacred.

I spent many weeks that winter implementing the instructions of absent teachers. Whenever appropriate I queried students about their education, particularly about their regard for its role in their lives. Most, once they trusted that my interest was genuine, spoke freely and thoughtfully. Some offered answers that suggested extensive contemplation. Whenever appropriate I visited with teachers about their careers, although I learned more from observation than from inquiry. Most teachers with whom I conversed were more guarded than their students.

I assisted with school functions, befriended a guidance counselor, attended senior graduation, and compiled copious notes. By the close of the academic year I was committed to eventually organizing and answering the questions that had been, day by day, gathering unrequited in my mind. By the time I had identified the two opposing answers—one right and the other wrong—to my primary question, I had unintentionally formed in my imagination a fictional cast of characters in orbit around those answers, and a story title with potentially opposite meanings.

The first edition of *Honor Student* was published seven years later. In the thirty years since, public education has relentlessly advanced the wrong, the anti-free-human, answer to my primary question.

That question was, and remains: What is the purpose of education?

Honor Student, 2019

In the spring of 1990 I received two unexpected telephone calls. One was from a librarian at Pinkerton Academy, an independent public high school in Derry, New Hampshire. The other was from a student at that school.

The librarian described "an unusual phenomenon." Students, she said, were not only reading a book that was not required reading, but "the library's two copies are being checked out and passed around before being returned, then checked out and passed around again." *Honor Student,* she explained, was creating conflict between students and teachers, and she asked if I would come to the school to defend my ideas in a lecture.

The student wanted to know what he and his friends could do to make the ideas in *Honor Student* a reality. When I arrived at Pinkerton to deliver my lecture, it was he who presented me to the assembly.

My theme that day was the answer to this young man's question. My goal was to illustrate the achievable connection between fiction and life, between the *ought to be* in art and and the *make it so* in reality. Although I may never know what influence I achieved in the lives of the students in my audience, the consequence of that day for me was the unexpected discovery of a word made plain by the gratitude, relief, and hope I saw in their faces—a word that described what I most wanted to offer readers of my novel.

The word was, and remains, *permission.*

Permission to ask the fundamental human question about any and every subject. Permission to demand a sensible answer. Permission to state with confidence and rectitude: "It is *my* mind."

That lecture is reprinted in the Afterword.

During the thirty years that have passed since *Honor Student* was first published, the world has witnessed unprecedented technological advancement and a nearly total dependence on—in some instances an addiction to—that technology. Collaterally, automatized minds are accepting a new reality.

Skyscrapers collapse at freefall speed into their own footprints after sustaining damage inadequate to collapse skyscrapers; America is at war against an enemy sufficiently ambiguous to assure politically adaptable targets forever; our government's heedless disregard for mathematical integrity has brought us eight hundred percent deeper into indebtedness; the word *friend* is now not only a verb, but a marketing device; the essential ingredient of a police state—presumed guilt applied to a citizenry of suspects—is all but normalized; human gender is a multiple-choice quiz with no incorrect answers; free speech is on the verge of drawing its final breath.

And, while funding a multi-billion-dollar security industry, American public schools more and more resemble physically the prisons they have long resembled intellectually.

The second edition of *Honor Student* has not been "updated" to reflect this transformation, for two reasons. First, the fundamentals of education have not changed over the past three decades, nor will they change over the next three. Second, revisions depicting an internment-center backdrop for today's anti-mind courses and politically correct behavior would make the book stranger than fiction.

In what appears to be, but is not, a cultural contrast to the aforementioned "reality for the successfully dumbed down," there has been an emerging trend in young-adult entertainment. Heroes inspired by values such as freedom, justice, honor, and love abound in popular literature and film. Despite, however, the resulting reasonable presumption that American youth still possess the capacity to admire individuals who battle oppression, corruption, lies, and self-renunciation, these modern champions can exist only in a reader's imagination or on a screen manipulated by legions of computer technicians. Correspondingly, the causes for which they fight become as detached from reality as their superhuman prowess and limitless supply of ammunition.

Fiction has the power to characterize virtues that can be made real in *this* world. It also has the power, by relegating virtuous action to fantasyland, to fictionalize virtue itself.

Honor Student takes place in *this* world. The struggle it portrays is real. The ammunition employed by its heroes is available to any aware honest person and is, without poetic license or Hollywood trickery, limitless. The stakes are not pass or fail, but freedom or subjugation.

In *this* world.

Despite alleged good intentions and beneficent trappings there is a mind-crippling contradiction inherent in state-controlled education. The system is politically manipulated, coercively funded, and intellectually bankrupt —and a Goliath waiting to be felled by the stone of unindoctrinated inquiry. Were students to take that stone in hand, were teachers to champion their charges' right to cognitive independence, "honor student" would cease to be an institutional stamp of approval on those who best conform to scaled cookie-cutter standards. It would become instead a personal badge, privately earned and owned for life by students who choose to think for themselves.

When that happens, this novel's epilogue will reflect in reality the properly human answer to the question: What is the purpose of education?

Michael Russell
November 2019

HONOR STUDENT

I

PREMISES

HUXLEY

*S*it down before fact as a little child, be
prepared to give up every preconceived
notion, follow humbly wherever and to
whatever abysses nature leads, or you shall
learn nothing.

Thomas Henry Huxley, 1825-1895
. . . *Life and Letters of Thomas Henry Huxley*

PROLOGUE

*H*e stood at the bow of the *Saint Sal Malone*, gazing fixedly over beryl waves into a sunset beyond his still-distant home port. Soon, the New England coast would materialize as a black thread dividing the emblazoned hues of sky and sea. Whaleback Light would appear as a pulsing mirage above the twinkling of dock lamps at New Castle and Gerrish Island. The ocean would grow dark and the horizon would pale as the light of day yielded to the lights of men.

November sixth found the heavily laden freighter returning to her port of call from northern Africa. Five times a year she docked for a week at Portsmouth Harbor. Five times a year one man watched from her deck the evanescence of the journey's last daylight, and always, like a witness to some ritual valediction, Captain Brevard Reneau looked on with unexpressed curiosity.

As he emerged from the forecastle door, his coarse white hair bending stiffly in the wind, he squinted at the familiar silhouette on the bow. It was nearly eight years ago, on a stormy midwinter morning outside a diner in Kittery, Maine, when the lubber had approached him for a job. Pale and gaunt he was, unaccustomed, Reneau had assumed, to even landsman labor, but the tone of his voice bore a certainty seldom heard and his eyes said his words told the truth.

"I have no experience at sea," he had confessed, "but I'll work harder than any man on your crew, and you won't owe me a cent until you say I've earned it."

"Where do you work now?" Reneau had asked.

"Islington Elementary."

"Teaching?"

"Sweeping."

"There are other reputable freighters in port—why come to me?"

"I once saw you fire a man."

"Are you in some sort of—"

The man's weary smile had anticipated the question and the captain let it drop. "How old are you?" he asked instead.

"Twenty-seven."

Reneau had guessed closer to forty. "We leave for Marseilles in six days," he decided. "You can start tomorrow loading gypsum."

By the end of his second voyage the man had surpassed in competence even the ship's most experienced hands, but he remained quiet and friendless among the crew, alone, save for the companionship of a leather-bound journal. He had been heard speaking Portuguese and French to the mixed-nationality crew, yet he stayed on board in foreign ports and his wages went unspent. When Reneau offered him the boatswain position at the start of his second year, he burst into laughter, joyless and distant. He apologized and fell into a brooding silence that lasted several days. Reneau never offered again.

A gull cried and the captain turned, pulling the door

shut behind him and ascending the steel steps to the bridge two at a time. He traded his brown oilskin jacket for a visored gray-wool cap hanging from a peg on the wall, then crossed to stand at the forward observation window. His fastidiously trimmed beard reflected the pink western sky. His eyes were Caribbean blue. Resting denim-shirted forearms atop the window's varnished sill, he watched the sun go down for Daniel Nolan, deckhand.

1

KEVIN SAUNDERS

"Why?"

The teacher stared. Kevin Saunders asked again.

"Why are we supposed to memorize the date of the Great Depression and who was in office when we haven't even discussed—"

"Because that's what's on your quiz." She scanned the room. "Anything else?"

Kevin looked beyond her to the blackboard and the list of answers to tomorrow's mix-and-match quiz.

"Very well," she said, brushing chalk dust from her right hand. "You may have the rest of the period to study. *Quietly.*"

Kevin recalled a day when the students of his ninth-grade Social Studies class were detained after school and made to write a hundred times each: "We will not talk in Mr. Forbes's class." Afterward, when asked whether or not they had learned to be quiet, Kevin had promptly volunteered, "If there is anything we've learned from you, Mr. Forbes, it's to never talk in your class."

Three years later, that was the clearest memory he

retained from his freshman year. That, and the words of an angry man with dark-gold eyes.

"Mrs. Turcotte?" he called, raising his hand.

She recognized the voice and answered without looking up from her work, "What is it?"

"Why doesn't anyone blame the Federal Reserve?"

She fingered her pen and let it fall to the desk. She eyed the clock.

"For what?" she asked blandly.

"For the crash of 1929. For the Depression."

"Didn't you read Chapter Five? The Federal Reserve was responsible for mopping up and getting us back on our feet."

"But wasn't it the Federal Reserve that made deficit spending possible?"

"So?" She tilted her face toward the ceiling and shook her head slightly. "What are you asking?"

"You told us it was created so that banks could loan money indefinitely, right?"

"Right. To prevent dangerous slumps in the economy."

"How does that work?"

"Very simply: Growth in business requires credit; bank reserves are a business's primary source of credit; shortages in bank reserves limit credit availability and consequently hinder or halt business growth."

"Is that bad?"

"Of course that's bad."

"Why?"

"Because businesses *have* to be allowed to grow."

"And extending unlimited credit at disproportionately low interest rates in the form of printed paper backed only by the promise of future tax dollars is the answer?"

"What are you trying to prove?" she demanded. The

legs of her chair squealed against the floor tiles as she stood. "That you're smart? You have the—"

"I'm trying to understand how a currency with no tangible value benefits an economic system. It seems it would only cause problems worse than economic slumps."

She measured several seconds of nettled silence, then scoffed irritably, "Have you finished? You have the second lowest average in this class, if you were smart you'd—"

"Only the second lowest?" he asked. He glanced toward the back of the room at a mop of tangled brown hair on an outstretched arm, then back at Mrs. Turcotte.

"I suppose you find that amusing," she rebuked.

Something in his eyes made her turn away, and he replied to her back, "Not at all."

He closed the door to his room, then lowered the cover on his turntable and sat on the beige-carpeted floor, leaning against the side of his bed with his legs outstretched. The whisper of an amplified silence breathed against him until slowly, from within the whisper, there arose a deep electronic resonance. Like a gentle current it flowed upward, in pitch and in volume, for a half minute. The hollow haunting notes of a bassoon floated in and out and back until finally becoming sustained, hovering like mist, leaving in their breathy wake the faint tinkling of glass chimes.

"Sparrow's Flight" began.

Kevin's eyes were closed, his head tilted back. Sunlight, sliced by the blinds of the room's west window, fell in bands across his legs. He wore black jeans with a white Oxford shirt unbuttoned to the waist. A narrow leather belt stressed the leanness of his body. He tensed and relaxed, occasionally he smiled, as the music moved through him.

Afraid of Heights No Longer was Phillip Sparrow's first album. Kevin had discovered it three years ago on the discount rack at Concord's only music store. It was the cover that caught his attention: a simple pen-and-ink sketch of a man on a hilltop looking skyward at a soaring bird. Centered plainly on the unadorned back were two titles: "Very Much Alive" and "Sparrow's Flight." For the finest music he had ever heard, for his first lesson on the difference between talent and popular predilection, he had given two dollars.

As the second movement crescendoed toward conclusion, Kevin opened his eyes and clasped his hands behind his head and stretched beneath the ductile stripes of sunbeam. There was an auburn luster in his collar-length straight brown hair; his eyes were a shade darker and, were frequent first impressions ascribed to them, serious and aware. A fine gold chain glistened against his throat as it rose and fell ever so slightly with his pulse. He swallowed and waited. His breathing slowed and stopped and held.

Movement Two crashed to a close, leaving in its stead a tranquil sonic panorama of waves breaking beneath the crystalline voice of Phillip Sparrow.

> "Of my Self it remains
> The release of these chains
> 'Fore the journey I've sought may begin.
>
> "With this earth and all sky
> Each tomorrow shall lie
> As my vista for flights from within."

The ocean grew distant and the whisper returned.

"Kevin," yelled his mother from downstairs, "your father's home."

Mr. Saunders was seated at the head of the lacquered-wood rectangular table when Kevin entered the dining room. The man's gelled black hair seemed an overcorrection for prematurely aged features.

"Hello," Kevin said, buttoning his shirt. His father nodded.

"Michelle," Mrs. Saunders called from the kitchen, "I could use some help in here."

Kevin's ten-year-old sister trotted into the dining room from the den, swishing twin dark-blonde pigtails from side to side. The telephone rang and she accelerated into the kitchen, snatching the handset from the wall cradle before it could ring a second time.

"Ke-vin!" she squealed teasingly a moment later, "it's you-know-who-oo!"

"Please tell her—"

"Tell her he'll call back after dinner," Mr. Saunders interposed.

The girl returned carrying a geese-patterned blue crockery dish heaped with mashed potatoes. She placed it carefully at the edge of the table, then dropped into her chair with a dramatic sigh. Mrs. Saunders delivered the rest of the meal in two trips and, after handing her husband the salad bowl, took her seat at the other end of the table with a sigh that sounded exactly like Michelle's.

"Ed," she said to her husband, "why don't you tell us how the faculty meeting went?"

Mr. Saunders' mouth closed over a chunk of lettuce. "Same as the last," he replied, wiping a dribble of Italian dressing from his chin. "The agenda never really changes, except I suspended Eric Dawson and Stevie Cole for being drunk at the Halloween dance, and now Coach Brandt wants me to let them play in tomorrow's game. Otherwise, he says, we won't make it to the championships."

"What did you tell him?" Kevin asked, unable to keep the suspicious tone from his voice.

Mr. Saunders swallowed, "Well, I'm sure he wouldn't have asked if it wasn't for the fact that we have a shot at the state title. Normally, I wouldn't be so indulgent."

"You're letting them play?"

"It's an important game."

"That's not the—"

"I also made it clear they cannot play next week," he qualified, "regardless of tomorrow's outcome."

"Dad, they knew what they were doing and what was at stake. They agreed to the rules when they joined the team. You can't just adapt them to fit the drift of a situation."

"I'm not adapting anything; I'm being open minded. And Brandt's right—there's no way we'll beat Plymouth without those two. You, of all people, should know that. Besides, I'm not doing it for Dawson or Cole, I'm doing it for the school—and for every one of us who wants to see Capital City win the title again."

Kevin shook his head. "You don't understand."

"Wrong," Mr. Saunders barked, slapping his salad fork onto the table. "*You* are the one who doesn't understand. I'm talking about the image of our school, and about fairness to two thousand students who would like to see their team play in the state championships."

"So am I—but for the right reasons."

"Don't you go telling me about reasons, young man. If you hadn't quit we wouldn't even need Dawson!"

"I got a job."

"For someone with your ability that's the same as quitting. Who knows, you might have gone on to play—"

"I don't want to be a football player."

Mr. Saunders' face was crimson. "You're a damn senior and you don't even know whether or not you want to go to college! If you hadn't quit football you probably would have gotten a free ride to any school in the east."

"I don't want a 'free ride.'"

"Well, if you think I'm going to shell out the bucks for four years of college when you can't even pass Turcotte's class—not to mention that warning from Barrymore—you've got another think coming! Your brother was valedictorian at Capital, with most of the same teachers and subjects as you, and even he has to bust his ass to get a decent grade at Hanover. If he had your attitude he wouldn't have lasted half a semester!"

"We're not talking about Edward Junior."

"Obviously not! He never caused his teachers any trouble, and he knew how to get along with people. Did you ever stop to think that if you weren't so damn self-centered you'd have some friends? Christ, I've never seen anyone so antisocial. What's your problem?"

Kevin pushed his chair back from the table. "Do you do that intentionally?" he asked, standing.

His father arched an eyebrow as if to say, "Do what?"

"Avoid the subject of your arguments?"

"I'm not avoiding anything, and *you're* the one who likes to argue. Which reminds me: I asked Mrs. Turcotte tonight how you were doing in Economics, and she told me you're still disrupting class. Do you have any idea how it feels to be the principal of a school where your own son is resented by half the faculty?"

"Half the faculty shouldn't be teaching, and she tops the list."

"Oh, really? Since when are you an expert on who should or shouldn't be teaching? Turcotte's been with us twenty-five years. She has a Master's in education."

Kevin nodded, expressionless. "So have you."

"What is *that* supposed to mean?"

"Forget it," Kevin exhaled, walking around the table and into the hall.

"Where—" Mr. Saunders turned in his chair, tipping it back onto two legs. "Where do you think you're going? I'm not finished talking with you!"

"You never started," Kevin replied, too softly to be heard as he climbed the stairs.

"Don't you go making plans to see Angela tonight! I want an *A* on that economics quiz tomorrow, and you're going to stay right here and study for it! And tell her not to call during—"

"Dinner," Kevin said, shutting his door and reaching for the telephone on the nightstand beside his bed.

"May I speak with Angela, please?" he asked quietly a few seconds later. "Thank you. . . . Hi, Angela. . . . No, don't worry about it. . . . I can't, I told Mr. Anderson I'd close for him on Fridays. . . . Sure, but I thought your school was having a banquet or something. . . . No, I'd rather not. . . . Okay, what's playing? . . . Then I'll see you Tuesday at seven. . . . Goodnight."

He disconnected and went to his desk and pressed a switch at the base of an armature lamp. The fluorescent bulb hummed and glowed faintly before lighting at the release of his finger, and he sorted through papers filed behind the cover of his calculus notebook. He extracted a photocopied worksheet and pulled out his chair and sat, and with a pen wrote an equation in the space to the right of the first problem, then several groups of numbers and letters, then an answer. He reviewed the equation and circled his answer.

There was a single sharp knock at the door and his

father leaned in. "Just checking," he said.

Twenty minutes later, Kevin placed the half-finished worksheet by the clock radio on his dresser and changed the alarm setting from six-thirty to six, realizing with minor annoyance that he would wake to news rather than to music. From the upper shelf of a ceiling-high bookcase he withdrew a hardcover edition of *Spontaneous Combustion*. He untied and kicked off his shoes, twisted the knob on the small silver reading lamp clamped to his bed's headboard, positioned his pillow between his back and the headboard, and opened his book to a page marked by a scrap of paper.

"Aris knew at once what had to be done," he read aloud, "and like a spark given the breath of the bellows, his thoughts became action."

"—of the hour, Secretary of Education Albert Winfield has scheduled a press conference to reveal his plan for revitalizing education in America's public schools. Winfield told reporters yesterday that the public's regard for its learning institutions must be improved, and that the federal government will soon be implementing major changes in the system in order to guarantee—"

Sitting sleepily at the edge of his bed, Kevin tapped the radio's *off* button and reached for his calculus worksheet.

2

SULLY'S PAGE

*T*he gymnasium smelled like a pep rally.

"…and not only are we gonna to win tonight, but next week as well, and then—onward! Onward to the state championships!"

Coach Brandt's voice required no amplification, but someone once told him that the microphone made him look like a football star doing commentary for sports television. He wore an avocado-green plaid sportcoat, too narrow in the shoulders and too short in the sleeves, with a goldenrod-yellow tie. He was not a fat man, although he bulged above his belt and collar. His jaw was square and he intoned a southern drawl preserved after four seasons as a linebacker at Tennessee Lutheran University. Peripheral to his duties as head football coach he taught history.

He raised a stout fist and bellowed, "Gimme a *C*!"

Kevin looked up from his book.

"Gimme an *A*!"

At the students separated by class.

"Gimme a *P*!"

At the teachers posted near the exits.

"Gimme an *I*!"

Across the rising fists he considered pep rallies.

"Gimme a *T*!"

School spirit.

"Gimme an *A*!"

And mobs in general.

"Gimme an *L*!"

He returned to his book.

"What's it spell?"

"Capital!" came the reply.

"Louder!"

"*Capital!*" came the reply, louder.

"One more time!" Coach Brandt demanded with both fists in the air.

"*Ca-pi-tal!*" the students screamed.

He stepped back and stood beneath the basketball hoop. His spiel on dedication, determination, and destiny had gone as rehearsed, and he had announced that Eric Dawson and Stevie Cole were back in the game.

"Thank you, Coach," said Mr. Saunders from the lectern. "Although Eric and Stevie will be allowed to play tonight, it's only because of the special nature of this game. As you all know, drinking is prohibited at school functions, and offenders must be dealt with strictly. Therefore, I am announcing officially that the boys will not be allowed to play next Friday regardless of tonight's outcome. But," he appended in a jubilant tone, "Plymouth is the team we *really* need to beat, and we're going to do it! Right? So, let's bring on Dee Mitchell and the Crusaders cheerleaders and show these guys some Capital High enthusiasm. Unless," he joked, "you'd rather go back to class ten minutes early? Good luck tonight, boys! We're behind you all the way!"

A dozen cheerleaders hopped, skipped, and bounced

onto the polished floor like an emptied basket of green-and-gold golf balls. Settling in a half circle facing Coach Brandt and the team, they awaited the command of a brightly smiling young woman with a meticulously coiffed mane of red hair.

"Watcha gonna do?" she cried, arms and pompoms outstretched.

"We're gonna go! We're gonna go!" the girls answered.

"Watcha gonna do?"

"We're gonna fight! We're gonna fight!"

"Watcha gonna do?"

"We're gonna win! We're gonna win!"

The girls spun in unison to face the assemblage.

"Watcha gonna do?" they shouted.

"We're gonna go! Fight! Win!" came the reply.

"Onward Crusaders!" finished Mr. Saunders into the microphone.

Mr. Sullivan was a stocky soft-spoken gentleman in his mid-forties, about five-foot-seven with curly graying hair and a close-cropped beard. Kind blue eyes glinted behind scratched bifocals; the furrows in his brow derived from a doggedly focused interest in improving the efficiency of anything mechanical. Standing before his students in a white canvas apron and brown linen tie, he looked not like a mechanic, but like a physicist. To his left, mounted chest high in an aluminum frame over rubber-tired casters, was a three-foot-square chalkboard deferentially known as Sully's Page. Seldom was the contraption far from his side in the classroom. A comment had once been made, and thereafter repeated with respectful good humor, that the dust on the tray beneath the board contained more information on the internal-combustion engine than any textbook ever published.

"Engine oil," he said quietly. "What do you think you know about it?"

There were seventeen students in fourth-period Auto Shop; most raised their hands.

"Ron?" Mr. Sullivan invited.

"It comes in different grades for different uses."

"Such as?"

"Ten-thirty, ten-forty, twenty-fifty."

"And to what do the numbers refer? Theo?"

"SAE ratings."

"Which indicate . . . ?"

"The density of the oil. Ten is thin; ninety is heavy."

Mr. Sullivan turned and printed *viscosity* on the board. "Who can tell me what it means?" he asked. "Kevin?"

"It's the degree of fluidity of a liquid."

"Good. More specifically, it refers to the *internal friction* of a fluid. But what should we know about engine oil before concerning ourselves with its grades?"

"Its purpose," said Keven matter-of-factly.

"And what is its purpose?"

Every student raised a hand except Dana Brissette, an unassuming dark-haired boy with the highest grade-point average in school. Dana's father, a mechanic employed by a car dealership in Hooksett, had insisted Dana take the class because, he had explained, his son needed to show interest in masculine work.

"Dana?" called Mr. Sullivan.

"Yes, sir?" Dana answered, removing his glasses and glancing around the room at the descending hands. He sat straighter in his chair when his eyes met Kevin's.

"What is the purpose of engine oil?"

"To reduce friction?" he suggested.

"Friction where? Caused by what?"

"Caused by the motor?"

"By the moving parts inside the motor. Okay?"

Dana nodded.

"Blake," Mr. Sullivan called, "does it serve any other purpose?"

Horace Blake worked afternoons at the shop where Dana's father was employed. He preferred not to be called by his first name.

"Sure," he replied, "it works as a seal for the pistons and rings."

"Very good, and very important. There are two—"

"Mr. Sullivan?" Blake interrupted.

"Yes?"

"I wasn't finished."

"I'm sorry. Please continue."

"Uh," Blake paused, bringing his hand to his chin. "What was my first answer?"

Smiles appeared throughout the room, but no one laughed.

"You said it works as a seal."

"Right. Thanks. It works as a seal and it helps cool the engine by circulating inside it."

"Very good. Is there—"

"It also washes away metal particles that could wear the engine faster."

Mr. Sullivan folded his arms and smiled. "Anything else?" he quipped good-naturedly.

Blake shook his head and flashed a waggish grin.

"Okay," said Mr. Sullivan, raising his voice to the class, "listen up. *SAE* is the acronym for Society of Automotive Engineers. *Viscosity* is the property of a fluid that allows it to maintain an amount of internal stress while continuing to resist excessive flow. Imagine that a cup of unused motor oil is actually billions of microscopic . . ."

When the end-of-period bell rang, Mr. Sullivan asked Kevin and Dana to come to his office, a cramped partitioned afterthought at the back of the room. Kevin took one of two seats against the wall; Dana stood, books in hand, near the door.

"Last weekend," said Mr. Sullivan, stepping sideways into the space behind his desk, "I offered to grade some biology tests for Mr. Theodore. His wife, you may have heard, just had a baby. I was up until two o'clock Saturday morning reading the darn things. You know, if students paid for school out of their own pockets, if they expected some practical return on their investment, this business of passing merely for the sake of passing might lose its appeal. Since that's not the way it works, however, even with an elective like mine, I have an idea. I'd appreciate your input."

"Sure," said Dana cheerfully.

"For every standard test given, an advanced version could be offered as an alternative. Each would be graded against a fixed degree-of-difficulty factor: one-point-zero for the required version, or 'Basic;' one-point-three for the optional, or 'Comprehensive.' In other words, each of ten questions on the Basic would be worth ten points, while each of ten questions on the Comprehensive would be worth thirteen, making a total possible score of a hundred and thirty.

"Here," he said, taking up a sheet of paper from his desk, "I've written some examples. In this class," he continued, referring to the paper, "a question on the Basic might read, 'Should a lighter- or heavier-weight motor oil be used in a high-mileage car?' The corresponding question on the Comprehensive would be, 'Define oil viscosity and describe how it relates to an internal-combustion engine.' In English, 'List the elements of concise composition,' and, 'Explain the nature and importance of concise composition.' In History, I don't know, but the Basic might ask, 'Describe the events leading to the American Revolution,' while the Comprehensive would ask that and, 'What likenesses can be seen between the causes of those events and the causes of contemporary political problems?'

"In other words, nothing would change for students who want merely to pass, but students seeking more could be rewarded."

"Wouldn't that be the same as giving extra-credit questions?" asked Dana.

"No. Extra-credit questions are an addition to the test everyone is taking, and often no more difficult. I'm suggesting tests that require a higher level of knowledge on every question."

"Oh," said Dana. "When would a student decide which test to take? On the first day of class? At the beginning of a quarter?"

"I see no reason why the choice couldn't be offered on a test-to-test basis. That way the student whose interest grows during the course can set higher goals, although each test would require a commitment. If, for example, you did well on the Basic and wished you'd taken the Comprehensive, or if you failed the Comprehensive and wanted a chance at the Basic, it would be too late. Just like accepting or declining a promotion: even if you change your mind a week later, the work you've done in the meantime still counts."

He paused, glancing beyond the partition at the clock on the classroom wall.

"Did the bell ring?" he asked. "I didn't hear it. I'll see

you Monday."

"Monday is Veteran's Day," reminded Dana.

"Tuesday, then. Have a good weekend."

Dana said goodbye and hurried out to his fifth-period class. Kevin remained seated.

"Why are you asking our opinions of this?" he asked. "If you think it's right, why not just give the test?"

Mr. Sullivan smiled as if he had expected the question. He crossed his legs and clasped his hands over one knee. "I'm not looking for advice on teaching technique," he replied, "if that's what you mean. Actually, I've already decided it's a good idea—I just wanted to share it with someone who might appreciate it. I wanted to hear your responses."

"But shouldn't every test be the equivalent of what you're suggesting? Isn't the Basic just a watered down version of a real test?"

Mr. Sullivan tilted his head, then nodded slowly. "I suppose it is," he said with a sigh. "It's just that kids are stuck here, whether or not they realize it, and they're stuck with whatever the system happens to consider appropriate. I'd like to do something to make it better, something to inspire above-average achievement, something to help students retain and use what they supposedly come here to learn."

He shrugged. "It's frustrating," he said, more to himself than to Kevin. "And it'll take forever to get approval on this test idea."

He paused again and raised his hands in a gesture of helplessness. "I don't know . . . Here I am teaching tune-ups and front-end alignments when most students will probably never even benefit from the important courses."

His gaze descended and settled somewhere beyond the plane of his desk. For a moment he was silent, and within the span of that moment Kevin regretted what his questions may have implied, but Mr. Sullivan looked back at him regardfully and smiled and said, "You're late. Who do you have this period?"

Kevin returned his teacher's smile, reminded by their exchange of how much he liked the man.

"Mrs. Turcotte," he answered.

From Plymouth's thirty-six with a minute remaining, Eric Dawson passed for the winning touchdown, and Capital City High School's Crusaders qualified for the Division A State Championships.

3

THE DECKHAND

Daniel Nolan lay sprawled face down across the width of his disheveled bed, still clothed in yesterday's flannel shirt and khaki trousers. His right arm hung awkwardly, limply, over one side. Beneath his dangling hand, lying open on the floor, was the journal in which he had been writing until a few hours ago. A ship's horn sounded three short, deep blasts and he stirred, rolling drowsily onto his back. Suddenly, he jerked and bolted upright, sitting cross-legged and rigid in the center of the bed, gazing with uncertainty about the room, feeling for the sway of the sea.

He leaned and reached and pushed his left hand into the space between his mattress and headboard and unplugged the lamp on his nightstand. He opened and closed the fingers of his right, flexing feeling back into it.

Haphazardly stacked in one corner of his room was a collection of notebooks and texts. By an open closet door leaned a white-tubed telescope on a folded wooden tripod; beside it on the floor stood a yellowed bas-relief globe in a brass-painted stand. The closet was empty. The room's walls were white and bare. The windows—one to the east and two facing north over Portsmouth Harbor—lacked adornment.

He yawned and stretched and rubbed his eyes, then stood and walked to the east window. The vessel whose horn had awakened him was passing beneath the elevated midsection of Memorial Bridge. It was a refitted Dežhneva destroyer, whitewashed with an open deck and eight rust-red derricks. He glowered as it cleared the bridge and picked up speed, steaming seaward with the Piscataqua.

From the balcony beneath his window, his sister searched the harbor for the shade of gray she needed. The blustery coastal wind pressed against her, molding the silk of her robe to her slender form, tousling her shoulder-length dark hair. Her green eyes methodically shifted focus: from the girders in the bridge to the bleak morning sky, from the deck of a barge to the smoke from its stack, from the wings of a gull to the great piles of salt just up-river. She studied the towering speckled mounds, squinting, blending, transposing, and returned indoors.

Ten minutes later she stepped back from her easel, smiling at the fresh stroke of gray on the canvas.

"Perfect!" she declared happily.

"Good morning, Rebecca," said Daniel, standing shirtless in the hall, his short ash-blonde hair still damp from the shower. A scar crossed diagonally from his upper chest to below his sternum. The sharply defined muscles of his torso and arms made him look like a boxer, she thought, or a labor-camp prisoner, as if noticing for the first time how his appearance had hardened.

"Good morning," she answered, setting her brush and palette aside. "How long have you been up?"

"Twenty minutes. I thought I'd sneak down and wash the dishes before you discovered what a mess I'd made. It seems I'm too late."

She smiled coyly. "Too late to keep it a secret, but not too late to clean it up. Or hadn't you noticed?"

On a singed towel on the counter in the kitchen was a glass dish encasing a brownish leathery rectangle.

"What was it?" she asked.

He chuckled. "Some kind of pasta casserole."

"How long was it in the oven?"

"I don't know," he answered, shrugging one shoulder. "I forgot about it. Maybe five hours."

"I offered . . ."

"I know. I wasn't hungry then."

"Daniel," she said, her tone becoming solemn, "why don't you ask about my paintings any more?"

He turned from her and stepped into the kitchen. "I didn't think you kept anything here," he called back.

"You know I don't," she answered, following him and leaning in the doorway. "But there are a couple in town you haven't seen, and the one at Schernthaner's."

She watched her older brother with a gentle intensity as he switched on the radio and began filling the sink with water. Once, briefly, he glanced at her, and for an instant she hoped he might respond, but his silence held. There was a time, she recalled, when he couldn't wait to see her paintings, and his days spent at home passed too quickly, but within the span of a year his interest in her work had died, and lately all but the most trivial conversation had to be prompted. At least, she thought, the fire of his extraordinary intellect still remained in his eyes, although more and more it seemed guarded or veiled. He could be indifferent about a subject that once moved him, or become enraged by something that never before mattered. She reached across the counter and lowered the volume on the radio.

"I worry about you," she said.

"You shouldn't," he advised, rinsing soap suds from a stoneware mug.

"How can you say that? Whenever I want to discuss anything of consequence you change the subject. Why?"

"What would you like to discuss?"

"History."

He set the mug in the dish-drain rack.

"It was once your favorite subject," she persisted. "Or have you forgotten?"

"Rebecca . . ."

"Please," she urged, "just tell me you haven't forgotten."

He stared into the sink with a faint and tired smile. "I haven't forgotten," he replied.

"Then tell me what you used to say about life and the passing of time."

"Come on, Rebecca, don't play this game with me."

The severity of her gaze was clouded with despair, but it gripped him, unwavering. "It's not a game," she said.

"Fine. What do you want me to say? That I'll go down to Islington High first thing Monday morning and fill out an application?"

"No."

"Then, what?"

"Nothing. I don't know. I mean—" Her voice softened. "I mean I'd like some indication that the time you spent as my teacher wasn't a selfless waste."

He frowned. "You know it wasn't."

"No, I don't, Daniel, not any more. You once told me that life was like a calendar, that a man could either fill its pages with plans and promise or leave them blank save the numbers given. Do you remember? I want to know that the pages of your calendar aren't blank, that you still have plans, that there's something you're working to achieve.

That you're not going to be a deckhand the rest of your life."

"Rebecca—"

"After Mom died, when you came to get me at Aunt Elizabeth's, do you remember our conversation on the way here? You told me things about our father I'll never forget; you made me feel as if I had known him. Daniel," she pleaded, waiting until he met her gaze, "what would he think if he saw you now?"

"That's enough," he cautioned. "You're not being fair."

"Yes, I am," she insisted unsteadily. "You admired him. You admired his refusal to quit when he knew he was right, and you said he'd never—"

"Shut up, goddamn it!"

She turned away from him and a single tear streamed down her cheek. She erased it with the back of her hand.

"I'm sorry," Daniel said tenderly, reaching for her shoulder with a dishwater-damp hand, his smile reappearing as tired as before, and sad.

She faced him again and took his hand. "Why can't you share any of it with me? You can't go on like this. You know you can't."

"I promise, Rebecca, someday I'll tell you everything. Okay?"

She closed her eyes.

"Okay?" he repeated. "You have my word."

She nodded, partly in acceptance of his answer, partly in acknowledgment that he was closing the subject.

"Do you still want to go out for breakfast?" he asked.

She released his hand and stroked the edge of his jaw. "Will you shave?" she asked.

"No," he replied, his smile broadening, "but I'll treat."

"Alright," she allowed. "I'll dress and be down in ten minutes."

He watched her exit the room and listened to her footsteps ascending the stairs. He restored the radio's volume and his position over the sink, but instead of continuing his chore he became still, his hands suspended over the sudsy water and his eyes narrowed as he listened to the voice on the radio.

". . . of Education Albert Winfield revealed at a press conference yesterday his plans for the revitalizing of education in America's public schools. Although Winfield said it would be inadvisable to disclose the finer points of his program at this time, he did specify that it would take effect in three basic stages beginning early next year, and he explained the critical need for revision."

"We are faced," said a dignified masculine voice, "with unacceptable shortcomings in our present system, and it has been far too long since any real changes have been implemented. Illiteracy, declining social attitudes, teenage pregnancy, disrespectful behavior toward figures of authority, substance abuse, and increasing dropout rates among students and teachers are only a few of the problems with which we are plagued. Until now, there have been no proposals innovative enough to strike an effective blow at more than one or two facets of the dilemma. I am, therefore, proud to announce the New America People's Educational System, the system that will, educationally speaking, put the United States back on its feet.

"Phase One will commence on January thirteenth with the selection of twelve schools to introduce our program. Public awareness and understanding will be our main objective at this stage, and there'll be an ongoing series of lectures, films, television specials, and community meetings. Phase Two, beginning next September, will involve full implementation at the chosen sites, but with a lenient, flexible enforcement policy to allow people time to adapt to necessary changes. Phase Three will entail the actual christening of the program on a national scale.

"We expect it will take approximately four years for the subtler benefits of the system to become apparent, but improved scholastic achievement and academic attitude can be expected by the end of the second year. Naturally we anticipate an occasional rough spot, but if everyone sticks together with the understanding that these objectives are in the best interest of our society as a whole, it won't be long before—"

With a violent backhanded sweep of his arm, Daniel sent the radio crashing to the floor. He gripped the edge of the sink, poised as if over a precipice, teetering in the strained, deliberate rhythm of his breathing. Slowly, collectedly, he walked to the silent box and stood looking down at it, then crushed it beneath the heel of his shoe.

"Did I tell you this was where I met Captain Reneau?" he asked Rebecca, sitting across from her in a patched-vinyl booth at the Wharf Road Diner.

"Once or twice," she replied, smiling.

"Did I tell you about the first time I saw him? It was in the fall, November, maybe December, a couple of months before I asked him for a job. I was walking on the docks when this giant red-faced sailor stormed past me and up the ramp to the *Sal Malone*. Apparently he'd just been fired, and he stood there shouting about how he couldn't work one shift because he'd had a hangover, and another because someone had taken his tools, and that it wasn't his fault he kept getting into fights, but Reneau kept at his task

—an inspection, I think, or inventory—ignoring the sailor, until he yelled something about needing the job and having kids to feed. Reneau looked up and said calmly, I could just hear his words: 'I'm sorry for your children that their father is irresponsible,' and when the man drew back to hit him he just stood there, waiting. The sailor lowered his fist and walked away, and Reneau went back to work."

"Why were you walking on the docks?"

"I sometimes—" he hesitated. "I sometimes just went for a walk on the docks. Last summer, twenty miles or so off the coast of Morocco, Reneau dove over the side after a man who'd lost his balance while repairing a damaged rail. It's a long way down, and at full speed on open water. Everyone else stood and watched."

"Where were you?"

"In the water."

"You mean . . . ?"

He laughed and nodded sheepishly.

"He must like you very much."

"I wonder sometimes what he knows about me. More than most, I suspect."

"Don't the two of you talk?"

"No. What ever became of that fiddle player? Harvey? Henry? What was his name?"

Rebecca frowned. "Hartley. And he's a violinist."

"Hartley. Right. You're not still seeing him, are you?"

She didn't answer.

"Are you?" he asked again.

"When I feel like it. Not often."

"Well . . . as long as he doesn't move in on you."

"He's spent the night a few times."

"Come on, Rebecca," he objected, "he's not worth the trouble. Isn't there anyone else?"

"David Keeler."

"The attorney?"

"They're both nice men and their feelings for me are genuine."

"I don't doubt it. You're talented, intelligent, independent—not to mention graced with considerable physical charm. Without you they'd have none of that."

He reached for his coffee and added, "You fill a gap in their lives, Rebecca."

"Has it never occurred to you that they might fill a gap in *my* life?" she asked. "Imagining being held by a man I've yet to know isn't always enough."

He glanced elusively through the window across the parking lot, realizing he should at least tell her he understood. Between the back end of a car and the hood of a pickup truck he could just make out a scattering of white-caps in the harbor. He sipped his coffee and found it luke-warm.

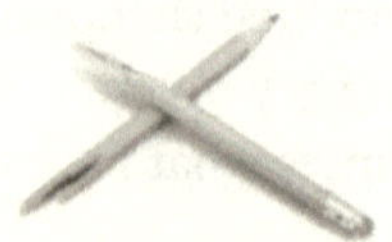

The frosty air nipped at Kevin's ears and face, stinging, bringing icy tears to his eyes and chilling the sweat on his neck and brow as he leaned into the final curve of a blurred decent. Directly ahead, beyond the level stretch of elevated pavement bisecting Oxbow Pond, Ruggles Hill towered like a wall, stalwart and grim against the cloudy morning sky.

He looked up at it, smiling defiantly, and pedaled faster.

4

THE EXPEDIENT AND THE APPROXIMATE

Dr. Wini Minkler held more awards for her work in student guidance than any other counselor in New England. She was Chairperson of the Concord Chapter of New Hampshire Women in Education, founder of the Capital City College Encouragement Club, and a special adviser to the Governor's Council of Students for Progressive Social Achievement. The wall behind her desk displayed an assortment of plaques and certificates, an enlarged color photograph of her prize-winning Pekingese, and a framed newspaper clipping overlain with a snapshot of the governor shaking her hand. She was a compact fidgety woman with evasive eyes and a tendency to whine.

Seated across from her at the round table in the center of her office was Mr. Saunders, staring wearily at an extra crease ironed into his trousers. Dr. Minkler browsed the pages of a psychology journal. Neither looked up when Mrs. Turcotte entered the room.

"Thank you for meeting with me on such short notice," she said, closing the door softly. "Third period is really my only free time, and I just had to get this thing settled before handing back the rest of the papers so as not to disrupt class for students who *care* about their grades."

She sat and jabbed a finger at the sheet of paper on the table between Dr. Minkler and Mr. Saunders. "This," she said with annoyed emphasis, "is not a true-or-false quiz. And he knows it."

Mr. Saunders smoothed his palm over his thigh and leaned forward as if studying the paper for the first time. His head rotated slowly from side to side, also not for the first time, when he reached Kevin's answers printed in blue ink across the bottom.

Pd. 5 Economics/Mrs. Turcotte

Match the following using the space provided below.

1) The Great Depression began in: A) Federal Reserve

2) Antitrust laws help protect: B) N.I.R.A.

3) The President in 1929 was: C) Socialist

4) England's economic system is: D) Roosevelt

5) The U.S. economic system is: E) The Consumer

6) Another economic system is: F) Public Utilities

7) Government-regulated business: G) Capitalism

8) Helped end the Depression: H) 1929

9) Nat'l Industrial Recovery Act: I) Hoover

10) Fostered the New Deal: J) Communism

1) *TRUE* 2) *FALSE* 3) *TRUE* 4) *FALSE* 5) *TRUE*

6) *TRUE* 7) *FALSE* 8) *FALSE* 9) *FALSE* 10) *PROBABLY*

"I don't know what to tell you, Marilyn," he said, turning the quiz face down on the table. "I've tried talking with him, but he just argues and walks away. I never had any problems with his brother. You remember Edward . . . he never caused you any trouble. As I recall, he was one of your favorites."

"Of course I remember Edward. He was one student a teacher could be proud of, and I'm not taking that away from you, but Kevin's altogether a different story and I won't put up with any more of his back talk. I can't. He only does it to antagonize me. He doesn't care whether or not—"

"Ed," Dr. Minkler cut in, "have you had complaints from his other teachers?"

"Not really. Not this year. Though he did get a warning from Miss Barrymore."

"*Mizz* Barrymore. Was that in Biology?"

"Environmental Studies."

"Pardon me," Mrs. Turcotte interjected. She leaned forward over the table. "I can sympathize with any teacher who has Kevin in class, but I'm here to discuss *my* class. Economics happens to be a very important subject, and if a student isn't willing to take it seriously, he—or she—" she modified, glancing at Dr. Minkler, "should not be wasting my time."

She sank back into her chair and folded her arms.

"I understand Kevin is doing well in Auto Shop and Calculus. Is that right, Ed?" Dr. Minkler asked.

"Yes. Very well."

"Then that rules out two of the most obvious theories as to why he might turn in a paper like this. One, that he has a problem with assignments requiring memorization. Two, that he is primarily mechanically inclined. Since he's scoring well on calculus exams he must have some ability to memorize, and it's obviously a subject that requires little mechanical aptitude."

"You don't think he's cheating in Calculus, do you?" Mr. Saunders asked apprehensively.

"With VanAnglin? No way. With Jennings or Martin maybe, but not with VanAnglin—he'd never get away with it. No," she said rising and stepping back from the table, "the problem is not so simple as cheating."

"What do you think it can be?"

She walked to her desk. She neatened a stack of papers. She propped herself at an ungainly angle against the desktop, leaning on her left hip and hand.

"It's not what I *think*, Ed," she began. "We're dealing with the actions of a seventeen-year-old male—no longer a boy, but not yet a man—who is very confused about his place in life and society. One can't *think* about an issue where the person in question is obviously unsure about what to think about himself. One has to *feel*. One has to get inside that person's emotions and experience the pain, the worry, the desire, the guilt—everything that comes with becoming an adult. Growing up is a terribly difficult process, especially in this day and age. You have to remember that Kevin is human, too. He has wants and needs like everybody else, and we must try to communicate directly with those wants and needs. That is, after all, the essence of communication. We must show him that we care, that we like him as well as any other student, and that he's equally important. Obviously he's not very happy, and it's our job to make him realize that that's okay, too, so long as he expresses his unhappiness constructively.

"Ed, Marilyn," she said, her eyes moving about the room as if new listeners had entered, "Kevin is suffering from what he perceives to be a lack of attention, and you may be sure that the deliberate defacing of this quiz is nothing more than an anguished cry for someone to recognize him as an individual. He doesn't want to do badly in class; he simply doesn't know how to show us what he's feeling."

She pushed away from her desk and began pacing between it and the table.

"Let's examine the whole picture," she urged. "He has only a few friends; he never attends school functions; he quit the football team; he deliberately disrupts classes; he spends most of his time alone; he's shown no interest in college; and he has never once been in to discuss his troubles with me." She cocked her head thoughtfully and asked, "Does he have a girlfriend?"

"I guess," Mr. Saunders answered. "But she's not a student at Capital."

"Okay. Well, anyway, he's not a bad person, and I don't think he's unintelligent, he just wants to be noticed, acknowledged, admired. Not for what he does, but for who he is. One might say he's really just trying to find himself. Yes . . . that's mainly what it is."

She discontinued her pacing and rejoined her clients at the table.

"And it's up to us to let him know that's alright," she summarized. "My suggestion is that you both make an effort at showing respect for his opinions by being patient with what seems to be a poor attitude. I guarantee his behavior and grades will improve, given time. All he needs is to feel that you respect him as a person."

She rose again and went to her desk. She rolled her chair out and sat.

"I realize, Marilyn," she said in a sympathetic tone, "that this may seem like a lot to ask, but believe me, it's for the best. Ed, I strongly suggest you send Kevin to see me if there are further problems. Okay? You both know you can call on me any time."

A gentle wind stirred the pile of dry leaves beneath the ancient sugar maple in the Saunders' front yard. The harsh light of a street lamp fingered its way through the giant's naked branches, casting swaying serpentine shadows upon the yellow-clapboarded Victorian house. Kevin breathed deeply of the crisp November air, waiting, standing beside a granite hitching post at the foot of the flagstone walkway. At six-fifty-five a lustrous sky-blue vintage pickup truck turned the corner and stopped at the curb. He opened the door and climbed in.

Angela Wallace had dark blonde hair, long and luxuriously thick, with a face and figure the envy of most of the girls at her school. Although born in New Hampshire, she had lived thirteen years in a wealthy Los Angeles suburb after her father's career required relocation to California. A year ago, as a high-school junior, she had transferred from St. Catherine's School for Girls in Hermosa Beach to Saint Benedict's Academy in Concord. She and Kevin had met at the bookstore where he worked, and they had been seeing each other almost weekly since August. Less often, he suspected, than she would have liked.

"Why aren't you wearing a jacket?" she asked, feeling the coolness of his cheek against her lips when she kissed him.

"I forgot," he replied, closing the door. "I must have been rushed."

"Your father?"

"Let's go," he said. "We'll miss the start of the movie."

She pushed the floor shifter into gear and accelerated

into the street. Two hours later, in the cinema parking lot, she asked, "On a scale from one to ten?"

"You mean zero to ten," Kevin corrected, smiling. "Eight-point-four."

"You liked it that much?"

He nodded.

"Even the ending?"

"Especially the ending."

She circled her arm around his waist as they neared the truck. "It's still early," she said, resting her head against his shoulder. "Do you have to go straight home tonight?"

The rutted gravel road leading downhill to what had once been Pierce Bridge ended on a grassy bank overlooking the Merrimack River. Two stone-and-mortar piers rose eerily into empty space above the powerful black current forty feet below. Angela set the parking brake and shut off the engine, then rotated the ignition key to keep the stereo quietly playing.

"We're here," she said, drawing closer to Kevin on the cloth-upholstered bench seat. "Do you want to talk? You can tell me what you liked about the movie."

Her profile shone softly red from the lighted face of a custom-installed music system. He turned to her. He extended his left arm over the back of the seat and rested his hand on her shoulder. He wanted to talk with her about the movie. He *always* wanted to talk, he realized, about entertainment they shared or his job or school. He wondered if she could tell, despite his frequently expressed disappointment with his teachers, that he enjoyed school. He wondered if she thought he expected too much, or if she thought, as his father once told him accusingly, that he liked "playing the part of the cheated student"—which made him understand that he *was* being cheated.

"No," he replied, wondering if the questions he asked

in frustration caused her to feel like he expected her to have the answers.

She smiled and leaned toward him, her hair cascading forward over her shoulder. She straightened to sweep it back and slid closer on the seat and kissed him. After a while she guided his right hand from where he had placed it on her arm to the front of her sweater, then pressed into the concavity of his palm, reassuringly holding his fingers beneath her own.

His thoughts about the movie slipped away, along with unbidden replays of his reprimand for "vandalizing" Mrs. Turcotte's quiz. He found himself drifting into an dreamlike cognizance, a heightened awareness of the blended fragrance of perfume and shampoo, of soft lips, of the truck cab's falling temperature, of a song on the stereo to which he had never before really listened, of the silent river, of the heart pounding beneath his hand.

When it was time to go she asked, "Have you ever been with anyone? I mean . . . Do you know what I mean?"

"Yes," he answered. "No, I haven't."

She looked into the foggy dark windshield for a moment, then back at him and asked, "Does it matter to you that I have?"

"No."

She smiled, knowing that he meant it, and brought him home.

Even in the coldest months Rebecca slept with a window partially open for the air off the sea and the harbor sounds, but tonight she lay bundled beneath the covers, chilled and uncomfortable although the window was closed. Her afternoon had been spent walking with Daniel along the streets of Strawberry Banke, talking of the sights and of little things soon forgotten. He bought her a dress and earrings, and it was all quite pleasant until she reminded him that it was his last day in port and that he had not asked about her latest painting. At once he grew silent; within an hour they were home. The light in his room was still burning when she went to bed at eleven-thirty.

In the morning she would find, as always, a note on the table paperclipped to an envelope of cash for the rent. By noon, the money would be in an account she had started for him two years ago. Eventually, she thought, he'd have use for it; he had told her so many times that his job on the *Sal Malone* was only temporary.

She shivered, knowing that the cold she felt came from within. She reached from under the covers for the telephone beside her bed and dialed Hartley's number, half hoping he wouldn't answer.

"Hello?" said Kevin sleepily.

"Hi. It's Angela. I'm sorry to call so late."

"Is anything wrong?"

"No, I just felt like talking."

"About what?"

"I don't know . . . Nothing special, I guess."

"I'm tired."

"I know. I'm sorry. I was wondering, would you like to come over for dinner next Thursday? You've never met my father."

"Sure, Thursday's fine."

"Six o'clock?"

"Sure."

"Great. Kevin?"

"Yes?"

"What you told me . . . about never . . . you know . . . I was thinking, maybe . . . Well, we'll talk Thursday, okay?"

"Okay."

"Goodnight."

"Goodnight, Angela."

$$5$$

REVIEW

*W*ith Dawson and Cole out of Friday night's game, the Crusaders nearly lost to Division B's Matheson High. As Kevin bicycled past the school on his way to work he heard the echoic clamor of a scrimmage rising from the practice field. He glanced at his watch and checked for traffic and turned and circled back behind the school's west wing. He pulled a water bottle from his down-tube cage and drank from it as he coasted through the parking lot. At the edge of the pavement he braked and dismounted, then lifted his bicycle lightly onto the grass and walked it toward the field.

Standing beneath a goal post with a trio of cheerleaders was Dee Mitchell, her crimson hair ablaze in the morning sun. She stared openly as Kevin approached, and when he leaned his bicycle against the frame of the empty bleachers she donned sunglasses and began a stroll in his direction.

At the far end of the field, barking instructions and blowing his whistle at the practicing team, Coach Brandt strutted exuberantly in the package-fresh wrinkles of a green-and-gold sweatsuit. Kevin noticed, as he climbed to the second tier and sat, the big man's disapproving glare.

"Hi, Kevin," Dee called, appearing from behind the bleachers, smiling vivaciously. She wore faded bluejeans and a pink silk scarf under a waist-length white leather jacket halfway zipped.

"Good morning, Dee," said Kevin.

"Is this yours?" she asked, pointing at his bicycle.

"Yes."

"It's very nice." She placed her hand over the narrow saddle and pressed down on it. "Jee-sus!" she exclaimed. "Doesn't this hurt?"

"No."

"I don't think I could handle having my feet attached to the pedals. I'd probably fall. How many speeds does it have?"

"Twelve," he answered, turning to observe the scrimmage.

"I'll bet it's fast," she said, squeezing the narrow front tire between her thumb and forefinger. She touched the gleaming top tube. "What an amazing color. Is it green or blue?"

"It's called Celeste," he replied. "Are you interested in bicycles?"

She smiled, then shrugged and said, "I'm interested in *your* bicycle." She crossed in front of the bleachers and sat beneath him on the first tier.

"Why my bicycle?"

"Because I'm interested in *you*," she said simply. "Or hadn't you noticed?"

"I hadn't noticed," he said.

"But you must have seen me looking at you in school?"

Coach Brandt yelled, "Pass, dammit!"

"I've seen you look at a lot of guys in school," Kevin said.

"I'm just being friendly," she replied without offense. "Most of the girls think you're stuck up; I think you're just reserved. I thought maybe you'd like to go out sometime."

"Thank you. No."

"Is it because of that girl from St. Benedict's?"

"No."

"Don't you find me attractive?" She sounded puzzled.

"You're beautiful, Dee," he answered. "But I'm not attracted to you."

"Oh," she said looking at her sneakers. She kicked absently at the grass with a heel. After a moment she asked, "Are you religious?"

"Hey, Saunders!" Coach Brandt boomed, jogging past them along the sideline ahead of the junior-varsity team. "Does my ex-QB miss the cheerleaders?"

When the squad had passed, Dee inquired in earnest, "Why doesn't he like you?"

Coach Brandt's scorn for Kevin was no secret. Many of his former quarterback's best decisions on the field had been at the expense of Brandt's strategies, and he had been unable to conceal his relief when Kevin didn't return after his junior year.

"I don't know," Kevin told her with a shrug. He stood and jumped easily over the first tier onto the grass. "Have a good weekend, Dee."

She watched him wheel his bicycle to the parking lot, position it on the pavement, affix a cleated shoe to a pedal, and in a single fluid motion push away from the curb and coast smoothly to the street. She stood and walked back to her friends beneath the goalpost.

An hour later, Eric Dawson fractured his right ulna.

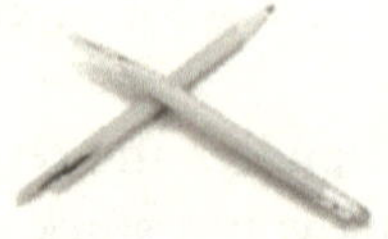

Angela lived in an expansive stone-and-glass house atop a Hopkinton hill with a panoramic view of the wooded countryside. Her father, tall, broad shouldered, dressed in the uniform of an airline pilot, greeted Kevin in the foyer. His handshake was firm; his eyes were vibrant and sincere.

"It's a pleasure to meet you," he said.

"Oh yes, Kevin," said Mrs. Wallace, appearing at her husband's side and taking his arm. "I've told Frank so much about you."

Kevin smiled politely. He had seen Mrs. Wallace only a few times in passing. She seemed always to be on her way to a luncheon or a meeting or shopping, and he had no idea what she knew about him through Angela.

"I must say," she continued, "I've been trying for a month to schedule a night when we could get together, but I guess we all have obligations and responsibilities. Frank's away most of the time; you kids have to study—not to mention your job at the library. And I, well, I'm constantly involved in one thing or another. Where does the time go?"

"Mom," said Angela from a wide dining-room doorway, "Kevin works in a bookstore." She smiled at Kevin.

"Oh, yes, of course. Is it that new one out in the mall? It's so big, and it has such a nice—"

"No, Mrs. Wallace," Kevin interjected, "it's the old one on North Main."

"Anderson's," said Mr. Wallace with an amiable grin. "Tom Anderson and I enlisted together. He used to read a book a day. I never saw anything like it. He opened his store with five racks of titles from his own library."

"I didn't know he was in the military," said Kevin.

"Air Force. But I don't suppose he'd talk much about it. He was discharged for— Well, I'm not actually sure what happened." He motioned toward the dining room. "Shall we? My flight's at nine-forty."

Mrs. Wallace hurried into the kitchen and within a few minutes had dinner on the candlelit linen-draped table. Angela poured water from a cut-crystal pitcher and sat in the chair across from Kevin's.

"I hope you like what we're having," she said.

"Sure he will," Mrs. Wallace proclaimed, lifting with a flourish the cover from an elegant silver serving dish. "This is roast Cornish game hen, and this," she removed another gleaming cover, "is broccoli almondine." She returned the lids and pointed. "Those are wheat-and-raisin bagels from Saul's Bakery, that's cauliflower polonaise, and over there we have stuffed baked potatoes with sour cream and fresh chives. Angela prepared the vegetables and potatoes—she's becoming quite the cook, you know."

"Kevin," said Mr. Wallace, "would you pass the bagels, please?"

Kevin obliged and asked, "Do you like flying as much now as when you started?"

Mr. Wallace nodded. "The advances in technology come so fast it always seems new, although being in the air feels the same." He paused. "What makes you think I liked it when I started?"

"Would you choose a career you didn't think you'd enjoy?"

"No, I wouldn't. But what about other factors?"

"Such as?"

"Money, lifestyle. I knew a pilot out of Montreal who never cared much for flying. He entered the field strictly for the pay."

Kevin nodded, then said, "And we both know a man who likes his business so much he doesn't mind having little else."

"Meaning?"

"Only that we have to choose our priorities. Ideally a person's career would provide for other interests. But I think," he added, "Mr. Anderson only likes reading."

Mr. Wallace smiled at the ease and certainty with which Kevin spoke. "Is that what you think I have?" he asked. "A career that provides for other interests?"

"You like your work and you probably make a lot of money."

"Yes, but there are . . ." His smile faded for an instant, then returned. "Is that what you intend to have?"

"Yes."

"Kevin," said Mrs. Wallace, "why don't you tell us what it's like going to a school where your own father's the principal."

"Mom . . ." Angela protested with an irritated glare.

"It's alright," said Kevin. "I don't mind."

"Do you think he's more strict with you than with the other students?" Mrs. Wallace asked.

"No. Not really. My father treats everyone with the same inconsistent flexibility."

"I see," said Mrs. Wallace. She frowned and shifted the subject. "I hear you have a brother at Hanover?"

"Yes."

"That's very impressive. How's he doing?"

"I don't know."

"Well, you must talk? Or write letters?"

"No."

Her eyebrows lifted. She glanced at Angela. "But he's your brother," she said.

"That's all we have in common."

She grimaced. "What a funny thing to say. Surely you must have played together when you were growing up."

"Of course."

"What happened?"

"When I was old enough to realize he wasn't someone I'd have as a friend, we stopped playing."

"Just like that?" she gasped, incredulous.

"I didn't like him all that much when we were children. And now we have no shared interests and entirely different ways of—" Kevin glanced across the table and saw Angela's discomfort. He did not care to explain further for Mrs. Wallace, but when Angela looked up at him he continued. "My brother doesn't mind being told what to think and do; I mind. Whatever relationship we have now is probably based on mutual tolerance."

"But that's such a shame," Mrs. Wallace protested. "Your own brother! I hope someday you'll be able to transcend your differences and get along with each other. It's no good being at odds with family, you know."

"We get along well enough. We just don't—"

"It's better than pretending your differences don't exist," Mr. Wallace broke in. His voice was quiet and even, but his words seemed formed with a remotely bitter emphasis. "A relationship held together by social duty and plastic smiles isn't worth a damn."

Mrs. Wallace exhaled meaningfully and said, "Okay, Frank. Would you please pass Kevin the potatoes? You do like potatoes, don't you, Kevin? Angela prepared those, you know. Angela!" she exclaimed suddenly, pointing with her fork at her daughter's plate. "You haven't touched your dinner! Aren't you hungry?"

"I'm fine," she said. "Is there anything you'd like to do later tonight?" she asked Kevin.

"I need to study. I have an exam in the morning with VanAnglin."

"Simon VanAnglin?" Mrs. Wallace ejaculated. "Isn't he the one who kicked the Davis boy out of class just for copying someone else's homework?"

Kevin looked at her.

"I know all about it from my parent-teacher group," she explained. "We were appalled."

"He also dismissed the other student for letting Davis copy," Kevin furthered.

"Unbelievable!" she said. She blotted her lips with her napkin and pointed at the platter of broccoli. "Help yourself, Kevin, there's more in the kitchen. Where was I? Oh, yes! We couldn't believe a teacher would get so upset over a little homework sharing. Most teachers let their students work in groups, and I think it's a good idea. It helps bring the class together."

"Mr. VanAnglin believes that mathematics requires a singular commitment to honesty, and he allows no exceptions." Kevin smiled. "He makes us do our work in pen."

"But it wasn't like they cheated on a test or anything important. You almost sound like you're defending him."

"Cheating is cheating, no matter how you look at it, and eventually there's a price to be paid."

"But it was only homework!"

"Mrs. Wallace, at the beginning of the year Mr. VanAnglin tells his students two things. He says, 'Two plus two equals four—not three or five or anything else. Mathematics is an exact science; being close doesn't count.' And, 'A equals A. Anyone attempting to evade the integrity of that equation by cheating will be expelled from my class.'"

"I don't know," she pondered dubiously. "It seems so unfair; they're just kids, bound to make mistakes. How are they supposed to learn if—"

"Is it unfair that two plus two doesn't equal anything but four?" Mr. Wallace inquired.

"I know, Frank, but the man could at least try to show some understanding and compassion. From what I hear he's totally heartless."

"His heart has nothing to do with it, Leanne."

"You know what I mean."

"I sure as hell don't," Mr. Wallace rebutted, raising his voice. More quietly he went on, "Those kids understood the consequences of their actions. Do you have any idea what would happen if I tried to cheat an approach at Washington National?"

"That's different."

"Only the consequences are different. It's exactly as Kevin said: cheating is cheating. Don't you think it's better to be slapped on the hand in school than drowned in the Potomac?"

Mrs. Wallace rolled her eyes and leaned conspiratorially toward Kevin. "Don't you worry about Frank," she said. "He makes a big deal about everything."

"Every day," Mr. Wallace said with emphasis, "millions of lives depend upon the integrity and responsible judgment of others. Pilots, bus drivers, car designers, meat packers, doctors, architects, electricians."

He paused and glanced at Kevin, then back at his wife. "I never thought about it until now, Leanne," he said, "but teachers especially. A man has to start thinking honestly and for himself sometime, and if he can't come to terms with that before leaving school he'll sure as hell learn it later the hard way."

He checked his watch, slid his chair back from the table, stood, and said, "I have to go. Thank you, Leanne and Angela, for a wonderful dinner. Kevin, would you walk with me to my car?"

In the garage, he turned and extended his hand.

"It's not often," he granted warmly, "that I enjoy such conversation at home."

Kevin smiled, taking the out-held hand, and said, "I'm glad to have met you."

"Your relationship with Angela has been good for her. She admires you, and I hope for her sake you remain friends long enough for her to understand you. She has a lot in common with her mother. In fact, she reminds me of Leanne when we first met, but I was quite a bit older than you and, well . . ."

He folded his garment bag into the trunk and set his briefcase on the passenger seat, then looked squarely at Kevin before continuing.

"A man's values have to be consistent in every aspect of his life," he said. "He can't strive like blazes at work and reach for nothing at home; he can't honor one contract out of professional efficacy and breach another because it no longer suits him. Liking your profession and being paid what you're worth are important, but so is setting and attaining goals in your personal life. I wish I'd known that at your age. If I was the sort of person to envy another, I might envy you. It's possible to achieve what you want and along the way meet someone who shares, right down to the ground, your view of life. It will be with such a person that you fall—no, that you *ascend*—to love."

Mr. Wallace's final sentence softened his stern demeanor, as if he had glimpsed something of import, but distant and melancholic. He ducked into his car and backed out of the garage under the rising overhead door. When Kevin returned to the dining room he found Angela alone clearing the table.

"May I help?" he asked.

"No, thank you," she answered. "Go ahead and finish

your dinner. Would you like me to warm it for you?"

He shook his head. "I should go home and study."

"Not until you've had some of my pecan pie," chimed a voice from the kitchen.

"Kevin," said Angela softly, "you haven't had a very good time tonight, have you?"

"Yes, I have." He rested his hand on her forearm. "I like your father."

Mrs. Wallace entered carrying a large slice of pie on a plate with two scoops of vanilla ice cream.

"There we are," she said, setting it at Kevin's place. "I'm afraid Angela and I don't indulge in dessert. Would either of you care for some nice hot tea? Angela, honey, why don't you fix us some tea." She winked at her daughter and confessed, "I'd like a minute or two with Kevin."

Angela collected and carried the last of the dishes into the kitchen. Mrs. Wallace sighed wistfully and said, "She thinks the world of you."

She pulled her chair next to Kevin's and sat with her hands folded primly in her lap. "About tonight . . . Frank, I mean. I'm sure he didn't intend to get so worked up about school and flying and all. I hope he didn't make you uncomfortable."

Kevin tilted his head. "Not at all," he replied.

"Good, I'm sure that will make Angela feel better. She's very self-conscious, you know, and embarrasses quite easily, particularly when her father's in one of his outspoken moods."

"I didn't know that."

"Oh, sure. You see, Kevin, Frank's never understood a woman's need to be treated with respect. You may have noticed his lack of regard for my opinions, and I don't think he's ever asked what I do when he's away, so it's important you realize how glad I am to see you treat Angela with respect. She may never have told you, but I know she appreciates it."

She patted the back of his hand, rose, returned her chair to its place at the table, and paused in the kitchen doorway. "I'm really glad we had this little chat," she said. "Now, you enjoy your dessert and don't worry about the dishes. I'll clean up later."

"Thank you for dinner, Mrs. Wallace."

"Oh, you're welcome. It was nothing at all. We must have you again sometime."

6

PLAYERS

Cybil Barrymore taught three levels of biology and a senior elective called Advanced Placement Environmental Studies. At twenty-three, she was Capital City's youngest teacher. She spent as much of her free time as possible organizing and attending environmentalist rallies, usually with a carload of students in tow. She had once been arrested for shattering with a rock the windshield of an excavator breaking ground for a building-supply store in a meadow near Interstate 89. The event had bestowed upon her a worship-worthy stature among certain students and school staff, and her previously mousy lectures transitioned into the militant assertions of a newly minted autocrat. Most of her students merely sought an easy *A*; some were full-fledged disciples.

The bell rang. The door closed.

"Good morning," said Ms. Barrymore soberly. "How many of you are familiar with the big oak tree at the corner of Route Thirteen and Clough Drive?"

A locker door banged shut in the silence.

"Come on," she prompted, "it's across from Oxbow

Pond. A huge tree—probably two centuries old."

It marked the beginning of Ruggles Hill. Kevin raised his hand.

"Well," she continued, "on Sunday morning, as I was pulling out of Clough Drive, I looked up to admire the late-autumn splendor of that fine old tree, and do you know what I saw? Powerlines running right through the middle of it. A whole section of branches had been cut away—I couldn't believe my eyes! One of the loveliest of nature's simple sights spoiled in the name of technology."

Her gaze flitted from face to face.

"How many of you have ever wanted to photograph a beautiful landscape but couldn't because the powerlines got in the way?"

A dozen hands went up.

"I thought so. There are so few places on earth left unspoiled by man. Everywhere we turn there's some un-natural eyesore: a powerline, a dam, a factory—"

"Do you have electricity at your house?" interrupted a voice from the back of the room.

"What?" she asked, realizing too late the source of the question.

"Do you have electricity at your house?" Kevin re-peated.

"Of course," she said, planting her hands on her hips. "That's not my point."

Dana Brissette leaned forward in his chair. He ap-peared to be resisting a smile.

"That's what I'm trying to understand," Kevin ex-plained. "What is your point?"

"My point, Mr. Saunders, is progress that destroys the environment—"

"Why with you is it always destruction? Why do you see only an eyesore when you look at a powerline? Why can't you see light, refrigeration, comfort, or safety?"

She folded her arms across her chest and said, "I will not be baited into having an argument with you."

"I don't want to argue. I want to know why it's bad to remove vegetation in order to deliver electricity."

"I didn't say it was bad."

"Last week it was that proposed off-ramp by your subdivision. Before that it was streetlights polluting the night sky. When I asked if you thought it was more important to 'preserve darkness' than provide visibility on sidewalks and streets, you said the same thing. You said, 'That's not the point.'"

"It wasn't the point, and we have a duty to protect the environment."

"Why is it always *the* environment and not *our* environment? Why do you make it sound as if we're uninvited guests on someone else's planet? As if human beings are unnatural?"

"I suppose *you* would like to see powerlines everywhere?"

"No."

"Pavement everywhere?"

"No."

She pointed to a newspaper page displayed on white posterboard beside the hallway door and asked, "Shopping centers everywhere?"

"That store—" Kevin began with ire coloring his tone. Dana turned in his seat. Ms. Barrymore cocked her head and pursed her lips.

"That store," he tried again evenly, "was being built on private property. The machine you're so proud of vandalizing was private property. If you wanted to protect a meadow from 'destruction' you should have bought it. Instead—in a show of who you really are—you threw a rock."

A pallor had replaced Ms. Barrymore's normally healthy glow, and Kevin wondered what was the cause of the twisted expression on her face. Anger? Or fear?

"Get out," she snarled.

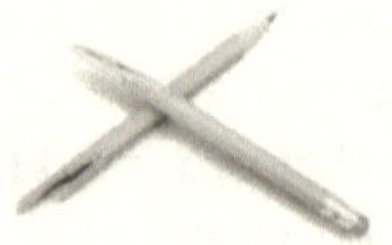

"You could have the best grades in school," said Dana, trailing Kevin into Auto Shop, "if you wanted. But I guess you know that."

Kevin placed his books on his desk. "I haven't given it much thought," he replied. "What I want is to learn as much as I can."

"And that's not always indicated by grades, right?"

"What do you think?"

Dana removed his glasses. "I think there's something wrong when a person of your intelligence is failing one of the easiest subjects in school. At first I thought it wasn't your fault, but . . ."

"Yes?"

"I think you're doing it on purpose."

Kevin smiled. "Really? Why?"

"I've been trying to figure that out. It wouldn't make sense to take a course and fail it intentionally."

"No," Kevin agreed, "it wouldn't."

"Then what are you doing?"

"I need the credit, and I don't think I'll fail. Not on my report card and certainly not in my purpose for taking the class."

"I don't understand."

"What difference does it make to you?"

Dana glanced away, his face slightly flushed. After a

few seconds he looked back at Kevin.

"You might think this is funny," he said, "but I admire you. I learn more in Ms. Barrymore's class with you there than, well, than I would if you weren't there. But I'm pretty sure you're not there to make it better for me or anyone else."

"I don't mind knowing that might be a consequence."

"Are you trying to get Ms. Barrymore to quit?" Dana asked suddenly.

Kevin's eyes widened at the question.

"After you left," Dana explained, "she told us to finish reading Chapter Six, and for the rest of the period she just stood by the windows and stared outside. It was weird. . . . *Are* you trying to get her to quit?"

Thoughtfully, Kevin answered, "No, I'm not. But, actually, I wouldn't mind seeing *that* as a consequence, either."

"Then why are you in her class?"

"To learn—although not only about environmental science and obviously not *from* Ms. Barrymore. I've been reading a book at Anderson's and keeping a second set of notes."

Kevin pulled a black composition book from between the textbooks on his desk. He showed Dana the cover, which in a white subject box bore a title hand printed in black marker.

"AP Environmental Studies," Dana read aloud. "Version *Barrymore?*" he inquired with a grin. Kevin flipped the book over. A rectangular white label read, *Environmental Science: The study of relations between organisms and their environments*.

Dana nodded introspectively.

Kevin said, "There's a difference between a definition based on facts and one based on an emotional response to facts. I don't want to be an environmental scientist, but I want to understand our environment, and I like thinking about our relationship with it."

"What about things like pollution and wasted natural resources? Wouldn't you agree with her—Ms. Barrymore, I mean—that *those* are offenses against the environment?"

"No. The offense, if that's the right word, would be against us, because it's *our* environment." Kevin slipped the notebook back into the stack. "Look, if we were to exhaust or destroy a resource necessary for our survival, we could either devise a means to restore it, find or create a replacement, or go extinct. The laws of nature apply to everything in nature, including humans. One of the chapters in this book is about wildlife in cities. It compares present-day species to what was there hundreds of years ago—how some animals adapted, how others didn't. It describes changes in breeding and nesting, feeding and behavior, even changes in physical appearance. It doesn't assert moral comparisons between cities and tepee villages and beaver colonies, it simply studies the—"

"Kevin," said Mr. Sullivan as he entered the room from the corridor, "your father would like to see you in his office."

The bell rang.

"Now?" Kevin asked, unsurprised by the summons.

"I believe that's what he meant," Mr. Sullivan replied.

Coach Brandt sat at the edge of Mr. Saunders' desk. Blocking the light of the room's only window stood a tall fleshy man with yellow-tinted glasses and thinning long brown hair. Mr. Saunders smiled anxiously at Kevin and motioned to a chair in the center of the room.

"We," he said, "that is, Coach Brandt and I, would like you to play in the state championships next weekend."

His voice was unnaturally tense, Kevin thought, as if an effort was required to make his words sound effortless.

"Really, Saunders, it's a great opportunity," Brandt encouraged. "I mean, I know guys who'd sell their souls for a chance at this game—and to just walk in like this! Hell, it's a once-in-a-lifetime. And about the other day," he added, "I didn't mean nothin', you know that. It was all in fun. Shit, I even thought about asking you to join the scrimmage, 'cept I knew you couldn't with your job, and all. You always were a stickler for responsibility. If only the rest of the guys had your sense of responsibility! Is he like that at home, Ed?"

"Sure. Listen, Kevin, you realize how important this game is to us—the school, I mean, and the students."

"And the community," said the bespectacled tall man.

"Oh . . ." Mr. Saunders said. "Kevin, this is Mr. Lucien Butterworth, the Concord School District superintendent."

"And mayoral candidate in the last election," the man reminded. He moved from the window and slouched beside it against the wall, then began systematically to pop the knuckles of each hand.

"Right," Mr. Saunders agreed. "And the community. Anyway, Dawson's going to be in a cast for six to eight weeks—and it wasn't entirely his fault, either. Just one of those things, I guess. You know, a bunch of jocks showing off in front of some pretty girls. Somebody's bound to get hurt. Except— Well, why'd it have to be Dawson?" he demanded of Brandt. "And why now? He knew our chances without him in the game! Why'd he go and pull a stupid stunt like that? You should have made him be careful in practice, Bill. You shouldn't have allowed him to play so hard after a week without training. This whole thing could have been avoided with a little supervision!"

"Gentlemen!" Lucien Butterworth intervened. "This is neither the time nor the place. We're here to discuss the upcoming game and the arrangements necessary to get this young man in it." He hooked his thumb at Kevin. "Now, it seems to me—and correct me if I'm wrong—but it seems to me we have two issues to contend with here. First, eligibility. The New Hampshire Manual of Intrastate High School Athletic Competition clearly forbids the introduction of any player into any game unless said player is an actual present member of the team in question. Fortunately for us, Calvin here is a stu—"

"Kevin," said Mr. Saunders.

"Of course. I apologize. Fortunately, Kevin is a student at Capital, and he used to be, from what I understand, on the team. Last year, wasn't it? Now, the way I see it, if we can come up with a legitimate reason for his having been off the team until now, we'll be okay." He turned to Brandt. "Could we get a physician's statement saying he's been sick or something?"

Brandt shook his head. "No way. Every coach in the division knows he quit. Statement or not, nobody'd believe it."

"I see," Lucien Butterworth mused. "Then the only solution is to let him wear the other boy's—"

"That's what I, uh, we, were thinking," Brandt cut in. "They're about the same size. Saunders might be a bit taller . . ." He glanced at Kevin. "Yeah," he decided, "in the legs. But he could wear Dawson's jersey and lots of eye black, and he'd have to keep his helmet on. And the guys, of course, would have to remember to call him by the right name, but I know we could pull it off. He already knows most of the plays."

His voice had a lively ring; his eyes, Kevin thought, looked uncharacteristically alert.

"Heck," said Mr. Saunders, "even if a few locals figured it out they'd understand. They'd know he wasn't doing it for himself."

Lucien Butterworth produced a satisfied smile and exclaimed, "Indeed! I was sure we could reach a viable solution. The only question—and don't get me wrong, I mean no discourtesy—is whether or not you're sure this kid's as good as Dawson. I'd hate to go through all of this and lose the game anyway. I'm sure you understand my concern."

"My son happens to be the best quarterback this school ever had," Mr. Saunders retorted almost indignantly. "And he's in top shape, too, from bicycling. If he hadn't quit he'd probably be the best quarterback in the state by now. Everyone says so."

He looked at his son as if searching for interest or encouragement. Kevin wondered what his father saw that prompted him to continue.

"He's way better than Dawson," Mr. Saunders asserted. "You'll see. And while everyone will think it's Dawson, we'll know, just the four of us, who brought home the title." He sighed. His gaze returned to Lucien Butterworth but seemed unfocused. "It's been eight years since we've had a championship cup in our trophy case," he said as if seeing it. "In a lot of ways, this could be the opportunity we've all been waiting for."

Coach Brandt and Lucien Butterworth were both leaning into the room. Mr. Saunders placed his hands palms down on his desktop and pulled himself and his chair slightly forward.

"Kevin," he said with gravity, "you remember how

much you wanted to play in the state championships last year, don't you?"

"Of course," Kevin replied.

"Can you imagine what it would feel like to throw a touchdown pass again?"

Brandt nodded.

"They used to be *your* team. You'd like to see them win, wouldn't you?"

"Yes."

"Son," Mr. Saunders pressed on, "what we're trying to say is . . . Well, on behalf of everyone at Capital City High, we'd be honored to have you quarterback for us in the state championships."

Kevin stared in wonder at the pride in his father's eyes, then sadly watched it expire when he gave his answer.

7

THE PAINTING

"That's because my mom's a bitch. Jodi's mom's totally nice. She lets her do anything," complained a blue-haired girl with braces.

"Why should I fuckin' care what college I go to? I'm not paying for it," said a dark-skinned girl with a low-cut blouse and a butterfly tattoo above her left breast.

"I'm gonna get so shitfaced after the game I won't even remember who I am," boasted a boy with a crucifix earring.

As the field-trip bus lumbered east along Route 4, Kevin gazed through smudged glass into the deciduous gray of rural New Hampshire. Only twice had he traveled outside New England, both times as a child, and he could still recall lying in bed at his uncle's farm in Minnesota, enveloped by an extraordinary quietude and darkness, wondering if he was awake or asleep. He remembered deciding that since he was wondering he must be awake and that when he stopped wondering he'd be asleep.

Two years later, for his tenth birthday, he spent a week visiting his paternal grandparents in Manhattan. One of his fondest recollections was their love for the city, but another memory often returned to haunt him. On the morning of his departure, while waiting for his grandmother on the sidewalk outside a bakery, he saw a car broadside a man riding a bicycle. Without hesitation he had dashed into the street.

The cyclist, he discovered, was the oldest person he had ever seen, and although his spindly legs were contorted grotesquely in the bicycle's mangled frame, his gaze remained serene and clear, fixed upon the face of the youngster who knelt at his side. He seized Kevin's left hand in an unexpectedly powerful grasp, as if, Kevin thought, he was a friend he feared losing.

The moment lasted only a few seconds. When the old man's grip relaxed and fell away Kevin looked helplessly into a gathering of merely curious faces and grew suddenly, inexplicably, enraged. He lunged into the encircling bodies, kicking, punching, clawing, screaming words he had never used into a vacuum he had never imagined.

He could still remember being restrained by anonymous hands and finding himself crying uncontrollably in his grandmother's arms, unaware at the time that what he had seen in the old man's eyes was not acceptance or serenity, but the entirety of a life in its ending.

The bus slowed, groaning into a turn and jerking forward with a slip of the clutch. Dr. Minkler rose cautiously from her seat at the front and stood in the aisle.

"Your attention please," she called in a whining tone. "I'd like to welcome everyone to the Capital City College Encouragement Club's third annual field trip to Durham State University, and especially those of you who have only recently joined our program. We've just turned onto Franklin Avenue, and if you'll look out your windows you'll see some of the sororities and fraternities that house many of DSU's academic patrons. One of the many advantages of sorority and fraternity living is, of course, the independent sense of sisterhood and brotherhood that can be found in such an environment. Dormitories accommodate the largest number of students at this university, and off-campus apartments make up the next largest group, so you can tell just by the numbers that life in a sorority or fraternity is more exclusive, and not all students are accepted as residents. They must first pass certain criteria, the result being a selective, family-type atmosphere. Now, coming up just ahead, if you'll—"

The bus veered right, then sharply left into the school's main entrance, tipping Dr. Minkler backwards into her seat. She swore under her breath and snapped at the operator, "Watch it!"

When they parked in the lot below the admissions building, she collected her coat and hat and assembled everyone outside the bus, then stepped onto a sidewalk and raised her hands for silence. "Welcome to Durham State University," she said. "Some of you may already be familiar with this honorable establishment. Some of you have been here before—perhaps to visit family or friends—and are knowledgeable regarding campus facilities. If, while we are touring the grounds, you feel you may have information to contribute to the group, or a question, please do not hesitate to do so. In a few moments we will be meeting Dean Chadworth, and I want you all to be on your best behavior. He has a minor speech impediment, and I don't want to hear anyone sniggering about it. Dean Chadworth has been kind enough—

"Tina!" she barked. "Tina Whiting! Kindly keep your gum in your mouth. Thank you. At noon we'll be breaking for lunch in the Kensington Hall Cafeteria. Everyone has, I trust, their lunch money with them? At twelve-thirty we'll be attending a freshman psychology class, and you're welcome to participate as students of that class, but for heaven's sake try not to ask any immature questions. Finally, we'll be meeting back here promptly at two, so don't wander off. We're here as a group, we'll tour as a group, and we'll learn as a group. Any questions?"

She about-faced and thirty-four students followed her up the broad granite stairway to the red-brick admissions building. Midway into the academic dean's campus overview, thirty-three students remained.

At twelve-fifteen, in a quiet restaurant on a side street in downtown Durham, Kevin ordered lunch. He took pleasure in the occasion of dining alone and finished with just enough time to meet the group at the bus, but as he stood to leave he noticed on the wall behind his table a painting he had not seen when seated. It held him, spellbound.

Brilliant turquoise waves spanned the unframed four-foot-wide canvas from edge to edge. He could just discern, as he leaned over the table, that each wave was formed of diaphanous upswept lines—hundreds in blue, hundreds in green—cresting and clashing as if set in chaotic conflict. A white horizon bisected the canvas horizontally, transitioning skyward into darkening gradients of blue. Adrift in the waves, slightly right of the canvas' center and listing to the left, was an hourglass two thirds depleted.

A cylindrical brass lamp above the painting lighted, causing the grains within the hourglass to radiate a metallic golden luster.

"Like it?"

Kevin turned to see a diminutive elderly man standing in the doorway behind him, his right hand resting on a wall-mounted switch. He wore a three-piece brown tweed suit tailored in a style Kevin remembered seeing in his grandfather's closet.

"It's yours for half price," the man said, "it's been here too long." He pocketed his hands and, pointing with his chin at the painting, elaborated, "I thought I'd sell it when I bought the lot, but most people want sunsets, coastlines, seagulls on driftwood—like everything else I have. Personally," he continued, walking to Kevin's side and studying the canvas in earnest, "I think it's beautifully executed, especially the way the hourglass sparkles in the light, although I cannot say I know what the painting means. I'm O'Connell. I own the place."

Kevin handed the man the money he had taken from his wallet to pay for lunch. "Kevin Saunders," he said. "Will that hold it for a few days? I can come back on Sunday."

"Sure," O'Connell replied, "but don't you want to think about it? Most people—"

"I have thought about it," Kevin said, leading the man to the register. He paid his bill and left his last two dollars and change for his waitress, then walked to the door.

"How old are you?" O'Connell queried from a few steps behind.

"Seventeen."

"No fooling?"

Kevin shook the man's hand and said goodbye. That night, a few minutes after he arrived home from work, Eric Dawson telephoned.

"I wanted to talk to you in school today," Eric said, "but you were on that field trip. Do you have a few minutes?"

"Sure," Kevin replied. He pulled a chair from under

the dining table and sat. The room was dark save for a rectangle of light spilling in from a wall sconce in the hallway.

"I heard what happened with Brandt and your dad. I'm sorry."

"That's okay."

"Well, at first," Eric clarified, "the guys and me wanted you to play even if it meant wearing my number, but we've thought about it and talked about it and . . . Well, we know you're right."

He paused, then said, "Are you still there?"

"Yes," Kevin answered.

"Anyway, I think the guys are going to play a great game Saturday. Not for Brandt or the school or for their stupid quarterback. For themselves. I thought you might like to know that. I thought maybe you'd even come to the game."

After another moment of silence Eric said, "Kevin?"

"I *am* glad to know that," Kevin replied quietly. "It's not why I thought you called me."

"Oh. You thought I was going to . . ." At the end of a long sigh he said, "Can I ask you a question?"

"Of course."

"I was wondering, would you have played if they let you wear *your* uniform?"

"Have I trained with the team since August?"

"Well, no."

"Have I played eleven games this season, win or lose, with the rest of you?"

"No."

"Am I even partially responsible for your qualifying for the championships?"

"No."

"Does that answer your question?"

"Yes," Eric replied laughing. "It does."

"Good luck," Kevin said. "And thanks."

He arranged to leave work early Saturday evening and attended the second half of the game. The Crusaders played valiantly, holding Manchester East to a single touchdown but remaining scoreless themselves. Coach Brandt was issued a warning for unsportsmanlike conduct.

Kevin awakened Sunday morning before dawn, kicking his covers to the foot of his bed and stretching naked on his back. He had forgotten to close his blinds and the street-light glared intrusively, lending to his skin and sheets a porcelain veneer. A car passed; the road sounded wet. He listened expectantly for the patter of rain, but there followed only a familiar kind of quiet.

Hurriedly, he dressed, and as he bicycled through the empty streets of Concord in the growing light, he whistled Phillip Sparrow's "Sparrow's Flight," snowflakes tumbling and swirling in his wake.

"This one?" said Angela, facing the painting behind the table. There was puzzlement in her voice.

Kevin's anticipatory smile waned. He asked, "What do you mean?"

"It's . . . I don't know." She shrugged. "What about that one?" she suggested, turning and crossing the room. "With the sailboat and sunrise—or sunset. Or," she pointed, "that one, with the cabin on the beach. It's only twenty dollars more."

O'Connell leaned and whispered, "Still want it?"

There remained the remnant of a smile on Kevin's face when he answered, "Of course I do."

II

HISTORY

W E L L S

Human history becomes more and more a race between education and catastrophe.

H.G. Wells, 1866-1946
. . . Outline of History

8

WYSTERIA

*T*imothy Elliot Nolan owned and operated the only ferry joining Canada with the United States across Lake Erie. He had spent eleven years, including the first three of his marriage to Maria Vitagliano, working for the day when he could offer a service that reduced a two hundred-mile drive to a twenty-five mile boat ride. At the age of twenty-eight, with a new Myron-Douglas steamer named *Wysteria*, he opened the Erie Straight Line. Ten months later, Maria gave birth to a son.

The child was raised witness to the discipline and vision of a promising self-made business. He was inquisitive and responsible, reserved, yet quick to smile, and possessed of a startlingly well-developed self-esteem. By the time he turned seven he was standing proudly at his father's side on the *Wysteria*'s deck, collecting tickets and performing errands, watching and learning, feeling useful and important. With the money he earned he bought a telescope and a globe and a lockable steel box for his savings, and it wasn't long before he grasped the significance of productive effort.

At the start of the fourth grade, he and his classmates were asked by their teacher to bring to school a favorite possession. A drawing of names was held, and the children were instructed to exchange their property for one day. Timothy Nolan's son frowned at the name he had drawn. He raised his hand, but without waiting to be recognized he inquired, "What for?"

"Daniel Nolan!" Miss Francis exclaimed, feigning astonishment. "I already told you. This is to be a day of sharing!"

"I only share with friends," Daniel said simply.

Miss Francis held her arms outstretched to the class. With an assuring smile she declared, "Everyone here is your friend."

Daniel's puzzled look transitioned into one of suspicion. There was a three-foot-long white-cardboard box on his desk. He placed his left hand over it.

"That isn't true," he contended, glancing again at the little rectangle of paper. "Teddy Blodgett is a loudmouth and a liar. He's not my friend."

A freckled fat face in the second row flaunted an indignant pout.

Miss Francis said with stern emphasis, "I suggest you apologize to Teddy . . . right now. And then, then you will share your toy with him."

Daniel moved the box from his desk to the floor under his chair.

"Did you hear what I said?" Miss Francis demanded tensely.

"Yes," Daniel replied.

"Then what are you waiting for?"

"Nothing."

"Nothing? How do you expect others to share with you if you won't share with them?"

"I have my own things."

"Well, we all have to get along. Who has Daniel's name?"

Joey Mulligan raised his hand.

"Joey," she said, smiling sweetly, "you like to share don't you?"

"Yes, Miss Francis," Joey droned deferentially.

"And what did *you* bring to share today?"

From a green-and-white plastic bread bag, Joey carefully extracted a baseball glove in new condition. "It's autographed," he informed the class, grinning elatedly.

"That's nice," said Miss Francis. "Would you please show Daniel that *you* are not too selfish to share."

Joey paused for an instant, and then slipped the glove back into the bag and extended it to the girl sitting beside him. It passed from hand to hand to Daniel's desk.

"There," said Miss Francis. "Now, Daniel, what do you say to Joey?"

Daniel scowled at the glove, then at Joey, and said, "You should never let anyone make you give your things away."

"We're not *giving* our things away," Miss Francis exclaimed, exasperated. "We're *sharing* them!"

She crossed the room, slid Daniel's box rearward from beneath his chair, and delivered it into the outstretched hands of Teddy Blodgett.

Daniel's chair banged into the desk behind him when he stood and stepped into the aisle. "I bought that with my own money," he stressed sternly, cutting an unhurried path toward Teddy three rows over. "I earned it."

The smug expression on Teddy's big face lasted only a moment. He rose and backed toward the front of the class, clumsily clenching the box against his stomach and chest.

"Miss Francis said!" he protested in a jeering tone as

he ducked behind her.

"You can't take what's mine," Daniel continued, still walking toward the boy, "and you can't make me give it away, either."

He stopped when he reached Miss Francis, standing slightly to her left.

"I mean it," he warned. "Hand it back, Teddy, or you'll be sorry."

Miss Francis spread her arms protectively. "Don't you dare threaten him, you arrogant brat! You're going to learn to get along with your peers, and sharing is the basis for—"

Daniel took a half step forward and punched Miss Francis in the shoulder. Teddy dropped the box.

Christine Parker was Daniel's English teacher at Central Erie Junior High. Twice a month she invited her students to submit for extra credit an essay from another class. After evaluating the papers for spelling and composition, she would add one percent of each essay's score to its author's final grade. Her students ranked consistently among the best in the school, and Daniel couldn't help wondering why some teachers seemed to dislike her.

One day, in the cafeteria during lunch, she found him sitting beside an eighth grader explaining the usage of commas. The older boy listened attentively; Miss Parker watched, intrigued. Not only was Daniel correct in his explanations, but he employed his own examples. When the student asked, "What if I still get it wrong?" Daniel replied, borrowing one of Miss Parker's favorite assurances, "Errors in knowledge can be corrected."

That afternoon she asked if he would assist with the review class she gave every Wednesday after school. He agreed enthusiastically. Two Wednesdays later, he announced to Miss Parker and his parents that he would be a teacher.

At about the same time, Allied Rec-Vee Industries was completing the construction of a motor-home factory north of Erie in Lawrence Park. Eighteen hundred jobs were soon to be available, but from Dunkirk to Meadville to Ashtabula jobs were easier to find than to fill, and twelve hundred positions remained open after two months of advertising. Across the lake in Ontario, however, unemployment was critically high, and it took less than ten days to finish the hiring with Canadians. Work visas were readily obtained, but the timely commencement of full-scale production rested on Allied's ability to secure transportation to Lawrence Park for its Canadian employees.

Dack Hooper, an industrial-relations specialist from Detroit, was contracted to rectify the dilemma. He came unannounced to the office of the Erie Straight Line on December tenth, and with a presumptive air requested the expansion of Nolan's service to accommodate six hundred employee passengers on first shift, four hundred on second, and two hundred on third.

"No," replied Nolan flatly.

"But you haven't heard my terms," Hooper protested.

"I don't need to hear your terms, Mr. Hooper. I have no intention of running a twenty-four-hour factory shuttle."

"But, Tim—and please, call me Dack—we're talking about a tremendous opportunity here. I mean—"

"Mr. Hooper, you're talking about a tremendous investment of planning, construction, hiring, and paperwork that may or may not result in a profit."

"A huge profit!" Hooper guaranteed enthusiastically. "Unlimited!"

Nolan smiled tolerantly. "Dependent," he said, "entirely upon the success of someone else's business, upon the status of twelve hundred government-issued work permits, upon continued Canadian unemployment, and upon my ability to run a business many times the size of the one I have now."

"Yes, but—"

"Mr. Hooper, I was seventeen when I decided to build this ferry. I wanted to own and run it without debt and as close to single-handedly as possible; I wanted a family, and I wanted to be able to come home at night and spend time with them; I wanted to make a thousand dollars a week.

"Now, at forty-two, I own every penny and paper of my business; I make the decisions and sometimes sweep the deck; I spend almost enough time with my wife and son; and I take in close to a thousand dollars a day. This represents the attainment of my goal, and more.

"Plus," he concluded, "I know my limits as a manager —I couldn't run this operation on a bigger scale."

"But you could hire a manager for the commuter portion of your business. You hadn't thought of that, had you, Tim?"

Nolan chuckled and looked away, shaking his head. "Somehow," he sighed, "I get the impression you haven't heard a word I said. Why not start your own ferry?"

"We wouldn't know where to begin—and it would take too much time. We need service *now*. Besides, funds are a bit short, with the delay in production and all."

"It's obvious, Mr. Hooper, that your client failed to conduct adequate research before starting this project."

Hooper looked genuinely confused. "Does that mean you're not going to help?" he asked.

"You have my answer."

"But have you considered what this will mean to twelve hundred men and women without jobs? Have you thought of their families?"

"I have not. Good day."

Ontario's Minister of Welfare and Unemployment, Lester Twombley, was waiting for Nolan on Long Point the following morning. He was infuriated.

"Am I to understand," he argued, "that your fellow men are not your concern? Do you not care about the welfare of your brothers?"

"I am an only child."

"Figuratively, Mr. Nolan. I speak figuratively."

"I don't," Nolan retaliated. He grabbed a clipboard from his desk and a windbreaker from a hook on the wall beside the door and said, "You're wasting my time and yours, but if you insist on saying what you came here to say you'll have to follow me. I'm working."

Twombley followed him into the gravel parking lot while while attempting to button his open jacket.

"Perhaps," he called, unable to match Nolan's pace while fastening buttons, "your concern lies with the workers of your own country. Understandable, sir, quite understandable, but I fear you may not realize that if these positions are not filled, the Allied plant will have to close."

"It hasn't opened," Nolan refuted over his shoulder.

"I'm saying, if it can't open, six hundred of your own people will be out of work."

"They're out of work now."

"Doesn't that bother you?"

Nolan stopped at an eight-foot-high gate constructed of welded-steel bars, sorted through keys on a ring, and freed a fist-size brass padlock from one end of a heavy chain. He rolled the gate open and turned to face the

Canadian.

"What bothers me is that you believe I should risk sacrificing my business in the name of other people's inability to find or hold a job, and that you have the temerity to imply that I stand in the way of their good fortune. I am not my brother's keeper, Twombley, I am *my* keeper, and if my brothers had the sense to keep themselves, they would not have this problem."

"Mr. Nolan, I'd like you to consider my viewpoint for a moment."

"Why should I?"

"Well, it's only fair to consider the opinions of a potential partner."

Nolan shook his head wearily. He entered the fenced enclosure and pulled the foot-long lever of a ball valve inside a cluster of dull-silver pipes. He closed and locked the gate and looked at his watch. He made a note on the paper on his clipboard, then faced Twombley.

"You represent a faction whose foremost asset, as far as I know, is need," he explained with forced patience. "Based on that, I can fairly say that anything you have to offer—especially your opinion—is of no value to me. As for the subject of partnership, never mention it again."

"I am the appointed spokesman and representative of almost four thousand jobless workers across my province. I'm here to—"

"What on earth is a 'jobless worker'?"

"What do you mean?"

Nolan laughed dispassionately. "I mean, Twombley, that a man is either jobless or a worker."

"I fail to see any humor in this. You wouldn't think it funny if it was *you* who was out of work."

"There's a reason I'm not out of work."

"Yes, and your luck could very easily change."

"My *what?*"

"Need I remind you that your business operates with the permission of the Canadian government?"

Again, Nolan laughed. "I *own* this property, and I pay considerable tax for your so-called permission. I think you'll find that I've been more than thorough in the founding of my business."

Nolan turned from the man and started across the parking lot toward the dock. Twombley doubled his chin and narrowed his eyes.

"We'll see about that," he hissed at Nolan's back, fastening the remaining buttons on his jacket.

On April first, the Province of Ontario opened a park at the base of Long Point, designating the fourteen-mile road to the ferry landing open only to non-motorized traffic. Desperately, Nolan tried to secure docking in Port Rowan and Clear Creek, but his efforts proved futile, and the practical extent of his attorney's advice was to avoid getting into court with the Canadian government. Maria met twice with the mayor of Erie and once with the governor of Pennsylvania, and Daniel wrote letters to senators and congressmen.

The mayor and governor each recommended expansion, as did both of the state's senators and all but one congressman, who offered his condolences. Restively, Nolan acknowledged the need for a temporary shutdown, using the time for an overhaul of the *Wysteria*, laboring twelve to fifteen hours a day while Maria and Daniel cleaned, painted, and polished. The work lasted less than a month.

"She's as pretty as she was the day you bought her," said Maria happily, standing beside her husband on the dock.

Nolan stared vacantly across the lake toward Long Point. "All dressed up with no place to go," he lamented.

"Timothy . . . Is that what you think?"

He laughed softly. "Actually," he replied, placing his arm around her waist, "I've been thinking about Daniel, twelve years old and not a doubt in his mind about the future—about *his* future. He has the self-certainty of . . . Hell, I don't know what."

Maria smiled. "Of his father?"

"Maybe. Maybe when I was sixteen or seventeen. You know, I think he's infatuated with Miss Parker."

Maria laughed warmly. "I'm glad they're close."

"He told me last night that after he graduates from college he's going to come back to Erie and teach with her."

"Maybe when he comes back he'll teach his little sister or brother."

Nolan drew her close and said, "We both know this is not the time for family additions."

"We've saved enough. Even if—"

"Probably enough for four or five years, but I want Daniel in the best university, regardless of cost, and I'd like to be able to give as much to a second child." He paused and turned and kissed her cheek. "Your mother had you when she was forty-one. We have time. I just need to know that the ferry—"

"Timothy . . ." Maria pivoted to face him within the circle of his arm and pressed her right index finger over his lips. "I'm carrying our second child."

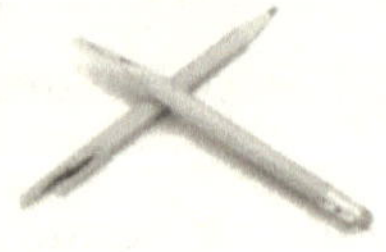

On the eleventh of May, Lester Twombley came to Nolan with an offer from the Province of Ontario to purchase the

Erie Straight Line. The proposed compensation was generous; the new Provincial Park was left unmentioned.

"Regrettably," Twombley said with no hint of regret, "it will be impossible for us to retain your services as captain. Why, you yourself said it was too big a task. Of course, even though we do have our own staff, you and your family would be welcome to jobs at any time. You'll find that we Canadians pay a pretty decent wage."

"What choice do I have?" asked Nolan tersely. "You'd probably try for nationalization, anyway."

"I hardly feel that would be necessary. Besides, your government would have to participate for such an alternative to be plausible, and that's not likely, is it?" Twombley glanced at the floor. "Hmmm . . . Although," he mumbled, "maybe if . . . No," he resolved without looking up. "I think it's premature to speak of nationalization. But, who can tell?"

"I'll need a few days."

"Wha— Really?" Twombley stammered. "That's great! Sure, sure, a few days will be fine. And if you decide to accept our offer by, say, the fifteenth, I might be able to arrange a bonus. In U.S. dollars."

Two weeks later, Long Point Road reopened to motor vehicles and Timothy Nolan's Erie Straight Line reopened as The Provincial Ferry.

Months passed. Nolan took a job as assistant foreman at a vending company in Fairfield, and although he never complained about the work he couldn't hide from his wife and son his discontentment. He bought a dinghy and went fishing with Daniel off the Presque Isle shore. He spoke of a trip to see the ocean and occasionally mentioned the possibility of starting another business, but in vague, spiritless terms. When Maria asked what he thought of the name *Rebecca*, he smiled wanly and said, "I like it."

Gradually, Daniel understood that his father was surrendering to an undefinable adversary. The intransigently independent man he idolized began to linger in bars between the vending company and home, secretly at first, but it was a secret soon betrayed by a dulling in his eyes, and week by week it grew more apparent in his face. He became lethargic, indifferent, distant. He never expressed anger toward Maria or Daniel, but insignificant concerns often enraged him. On the morning of his daughter's birth he wept.

The next day, an officer of The Provincial Ferry found him floating face down in the water beside the hull of the *PF2*, formerly the *Wysteria*.

9

DANIEL NOLAN

Daniel pursued his studies with an inexorable sense of purpose. His passion for learning became irrepressible; his desire to teach, unswerving and unquestioned. Little else seemed to matter as he moved from class to class and grade to grade on a solitary one-way track. When asked by a visiting relative if he liked senior high he replied, "I'll endure whatever is necessary to become a teacher."

Miss Parker's weekly after-school class remained his greatest joy, but even she found his temperament alarming. He displayed a boundless patience toward any student who genuinely sought help, but his anger flared at the slightest sign of apathy or resistance. When asked why, he replied: "If they don't want to learn they shouldn't be in school. An unwilling mind can't be taught."

Often he read through the night, falling asleep at his desk or in a bed littered with papers and books. He zealously engaged his assignments, and on the back of every test produced an essay on a topic not yet covered. His classroom demeanor was unforbearing, even reckless, and many of his teachers were intimidated by the intensity of his presence. He raised his hand for almost every question asked, while frequently his questions went unanswered. He made mistakes, although to everyone's astonishment he was never upset by them.

He would say, "Errors in knowledge can be corrected," and he would study harder.

He spent weekends walking the grassy dunes by the lighthouse on the northern shore of Presque Isle, writing, reading, thinking, remembering his father. Once in a while he would see the hulking vessels of the Provincial Ferry as they entered Thompson Bay, but by the end of his senior year at Irving High, Allied Rec-Vee Industries declared bankruptcy and the ferry stopped running.

He majored in history at Marquette University, and although his father had put aside more than enough money to see him through college, he worked nights for an air-freight company in Sands and paid most of his tuition. His personal relationships were few and brief. Women found him alluring, but the unsettling directness of his gaze kept most at a distance, and he seemed not to notice their admiring glances. At times, he wished he had a friend; consciously he disowned disappointment. Eventually he felt an encroaching loneliness, but at the start of his final term at Marquette he discovered a lively kinship in correspondence with Rebecca.

He delighted in reading her letters, so carefully composed, so complete in thought. The questions she asked of his life at school and the descriptions she gave of her own were extraordinarily perceptive. He learned that she never played "house" or with dolls, and that she had never been invited to a sleepover. Instead, she played stickball and broom hockey and climbed trees with the boys, often coming home scraped and bruised.

For her eighth birthday he sent her an easel and watercolor set, and every letter he received thereafter was accompanied by a painting, each painstakingly detailed, each displaying more skill than the last. His favorite was of a bridge done in fine black lines on a mottled-bronze background.

She had titled it, "Across Lake Erie."

"That was the shortest valedictory I've ever heard," called Christine Parker over the thrum of a late-afternoon rain, smiling from under a red umbrella as Daniel approached her outside the Marquette Convocation Center.

He grinned. "I hope I didn't bore anyone. Thanks for applauding."

"Someone had to! Where were all your fans?"

They laughed together and he took her hand in greeting. She tilted onto her toes and kissed his cheek.

"It's wonderful to see you," he said happily. "You look sensational."

"You mean I don't look like your old seventh-grade teacher?" she asked lightly, raising her umbrella and standing close enough to share it.

"Old? You must be . . . what? Thirty-two?"

"Thirty-four."

"You look twenty-four, tops."

"Thanks." She winked and added, "You, too!"

"Really? I'm only twenty-one."

Her gaze deepened as she searched his. "Not your eyes," she said just before he looked away.

"When do you go back?" he asked.

"Tomorrow."

She handed him a rain-dampened envelope. "From your mother," she said.

He slipped it into a pocket inside his jacket. "When did you see her?"

"Last night. She said you asked her not to come, but she didn't seem to mind."

He nodded. "Where are you staying?"

"At the Charlevoix."

"On a teacher's salary?"

"It's a special occasion. May I take you to dinner?"

"Absolutely," he exclaimed, smiling. "What time? My apartment's just down the street."

"Show me," she said, producing from her purse a set of keys. "I rented a car."

She returned to collect him at six-fifteen, and all through dinner he expounded on his plans. She had learned from his mother his decision to attend graduate school, but she listened, smiling excitedly, engrossed in the rhapsodic outpouring of his aspirations. Afterward, sitting in her rental car in the hotel garage, she asked, "Have you ever thought of me?"

"Of course," he answered.

"I mean . . . not just as your teacher."

He looked at her in the shadowy weak light, at the lace accenting her sheer high-collared dress, at the graceful contour of her long neck and slender shoulders, at her face and into her eyes, suddenly young and lovely and unknown to him. It was dawn before they fell asleep in her room.

He woke alone mid-morning to a letter on her pillow.

> Tomorrow I start my new job as a reporter
> for the *Buffalo Sun*. I have had enough. I'm
> sick of trying to teach students who don't
> care. I'm sick of dealing with parents who
> don't care. I'm sick of school board
> members who don't care. As much as I
> love teaching and as much as I shall miss
> it, I'll not be back. Never before have I felt
> so helpless. I can't even name what went
> wrong, and last night I couldn't tell you
> that I came here to say this.
>
> Goodbye, Daniel. I'm sorry.

Her telephone in Erie was out of service. Her Buffalo number was unpublished. He wrote to her at the newspaper but his letters came back unopened. For weeks he hurt and wondered and tried not to blame her, but he did blame her, and finally he swore to forget.

With a Master's degree *summa cum laude* from Vaillancourt, Daniel returned to Erie as a history teacher at Irving High.

It was not what he anticipated.

The contradictions he had ignored as a student, the apathy he had brushed aside as unreal, the senseless requirements he had deemed trivial while pursuing his career, loomed inescapably larger than life. No longer, he discovered, could they be ignored or brushed aside; no longer were they trivialities. Like a bridge spanning less than the width of a chasm their significance stretched before him as an absolute, and he groped for the means to manage them.

Twice he was reprimanded by the head of the history department for rearranging textbook chapters chronologically; twice he was chastised by parents for assigning too much homework; three times he was asked by the principal not to give tests comprised solely of essay questions; a dozen times he was rebuked for over-emphasizing spelling and grammar. Midway into the third quarter he was summoned to appear before the Greater Erie School Board.

"It has come to our attention that you may be straying from the duly established parameters of your U.S. History class," the superintendent began gravely.

"What is *that* supposed to mean?" Daniel asked, scrutinizing the seven faces before him.

"You are currently discussing economics?"

"I am."

"We're told you have spoken out against American labor unions."

"Inaccurate. I have presented historical evidence that labor unions are not responsible for America's prosperity, and I have—"

"Oh?" the superintendent broke in, bending the word and arching his eyebrows. "What is?"

"To the extent to which it has been allowed to exist, laissez-faire capitalism."

"Really, Mr. Nolan, isn't that a naïve and behind-the-times notion? And where in our approved textbook did you extract your 'historical evidence'? We don't want our faculty teaching outdated concepts at Irving."

Daniel laughed and replied, "We're studying more than one text, since our approved version suffers from amnesia." Wryly, he challenged, "Would you prefer I repeat fashionable platitudes? Shall I lecture my students on the fairness of wealth redistribution?"

He paused in awareness of his sarcasm and asked flatly, "Why have you asked me here?"

The superintendent removed a folder from his briefcase and, with a flourish, let it fall onto the table. "As we understand it," he replied, "your lectures contradict the very ideals of this country's economic policy."

"Which ideals? Those implicit in America's founding? Or today's?"

"Our sources indicate that you have denounced price supports, subsidies, antitrust law, the postal service, and the minimum wage. You've told your students that there should be no Department of Welfare, no Social Security, no consumer-protection agencies, no utility-rate controls, no government funding for the—"

"I've shown my students the historical consequences of government intervention in commerce. When someone asks specifically what I think about a particular topic, I provide an honest answer. I do not, however, tell my students what to think."

"Mr. Nolan—"

"Listen to me. The government of a free country has one proper function: the protection of the rights—the individual rights—of its citizens."

"Mr. Nolan—"

"It would have its military to protect against external aggression, its police to protect against internal aggression, and its court system to uphold the laws necessary for the preservation of constitutionally guaranteed rights. In an economically free society, those who seek value are those who create value. Safe, dependable, affordable, superior products and services are what we require, and the nature of a free market is such that products and services of inferior quality will not be sustained. *That* is what I want my students to understand, but not because I say so. In an objective presentation on the history of America, *that* is what students couldn't help but understand."

Silence filled the room. The superintendent reclined in his chair. He looked in turn at each of the men and women around the conference table. His mouth formed a tight-lipped grin.

"I do believe," he said through the grin, "that you have forgotten where you are."

Several of the faces grinned similarly.

"You," the superintendent emphasized, "are employed at a school funded by taxes. You are permitted to teach because your skills have been approved by the state. You are a cog in a wheel that turns in the interest of . . ."

Daniel no longer heard the words, but their sound swept over him like a torrent, howling in his ears and hammering at his brain, dragging him down and smothering him beneath the weight of their meaning. Aghast, he found himself staring in a half-bewildered, half-nauseated silence at the monstrosity of his guilt, engulfed by an inenarrable flood of emotion. He felt incapacitated and numb as he groped for control.

". . . and where," the sound was demanding a few seconds or minutes later, "do you think education would be without government guidance and backing? Where, Mr. Nolan, would *you* be?"

The faces waited, smug in anticipation of seeing such a

man helpless, yet anxious to grant forgiveness upon hearing his excuse. Ruthlessly, Daniel forced from his mind an onslaught of self-condemnatory questions. Purposefully, he recalled a familiar perspective. He swallowed, and his gaze returned to the superintendent.

"Errors in knowledge . . ." he began hoarsely.

"What?" asked the superintendent.

Daniel steadied himself against the back of his chair. He cleared his throat. "Obviously," he said, "I've made a mistake."

"Mr. Nolan, we only need your assurance—"

"You have my word it won't happen again."

The superintendent sucked in his cheeks and tapped his lips with the tip of his right index finger. "Well," he said, "that's good. That's good. You are a competent educator in other respects, and your students seem to admire you. I trust, then, in the future, you will stay within the guidelines of our approved text?"

"To the best of my ability until the end of the quarter."

"Fine. That's good. I'm very glad we—" He stopped. He glanced around the room. He looked back at Daniel and asked, "What do you mean, 'until the end of the quarter'?"

Daniel loosened his tie and unbuttoned the collar of his shirt. "Find a replacement," he said.

"But didn't you just tell us—"

"That I made a mistake."

"Yes."

"I'm about to correct it."

"By quitting?"

"By acknowledging my failure to question the thing most important to me. By acknowledging my failure to recognize the contradiction of it. By applying to an essential product the principles of the only economic system that recognizes individual rights. Education belongs on the free market."

The superintendent's face seemed to lengthen. "That is the most asinine thing I've ever heard," he blurted. "How the hell is a school system going to function *as a business*? The only thing businessmen understand is profit."

"Which means, net gain over investment. Wouldn't you say that students who acquire the knowledge necessary to lead happy, productive lives are profiting?"

"Theoretically, sure, but that's not how businessmen would see it. The only thing they understand is money."

"Money, in a wholly capitalist society, is simply a medium of trade created by the best in men: by their intelligence, their ability, their productive effort. Don't boast too loudly your contempt for money. Respect for what it represents comes only to those who have earned it."

The superintendent drew back. "What are you insinuating?"

"Nothing. We were discussing the private ownership of schools."

"*You* were discussing it. I already know it wouldn't work. There are plenty of parents who'd like to see their kids in a private school. Not everyone can afford it."

"Partly because they're forced to pay for public education. Partly because the market is too restricted for competitive tuition. That would change under free-market conditions."

Daniel couldn't help smiling. The argument—no, he thought, the *principle*—was universal.

"And who would control the standard of education, if not the government?" the superintendent asked.

"Consumers of every product seek high quality at a competitive price, whether they're shopping for groceries or a home . . . or an education. Schools that offer the best teachers, subjects, and tuition will attract customers and remain in business. Quality will prevail."

"Uh-huh. And how would you get kids to go to school? Assuming, of course, no truancy laws."

"You can force a child to attend a school, but you cannot force him to learn, which is his reason for being there. You can condition a child to repeat what you tell him, but you cannot make him think it. Since parents have a moral obligation to provide for their children's development, children would attend school in accordance with their parents' choice."

"What about children whose parents don't care?"

Daniel shrugged. "They're in school now only because the law requires it, neither questioning nor learning, eventually quitting or graduating no more educated than when they began."

"Maybe . . . But what happens when a family can't pay tuition even at the cheapest school? What about *their* children's education?"

"You mean, who's going to rescue the children of parents who disassociate thinking from baby-making? It's a shame there are such parents, but forcing the care of their children on conscientious parents is a greater injustice. Scholarships and financial aid would no doubt be available from private sources, like any charity dependent on voluntary contributions."

"Are you suggesting *no* government funding at all? Not even grants, or loans, or—"

"None."

"Not even locally?"

"Not at any level."

"That's insane!" It was almost a shriek. "The poor need schooling, too! Imagine education being *sold* by a bunch of money-grubbing executives! Look at us!" he cried to the board. "Talking about schools as if they were some damn retail commodity. We're educators, Nolan, not car dealers. What you suggest would ruin America intellectually. And it's downright *un*-American to make the less fortunate have to fend for themselves."

"On the contrary, the entrenched assumption that parents must deliver their children into *any* government-controlled institution derives from another political theory entirely."

Daniel's words came without effort or pause, clearly and precisely, as if he had articulated them a hundred times. He didn't realize he was standing.

"As for America intellectually," he continued, "open your eyes. Have you not seen what our educational system produces? Have you not noticed the conceptual helplessness of the average high-school graduate? Have you never wondered why young cashiers and clerks and summer help can't add or write or speak or think? Do you not suspect that their need for drug- and alcohol-induced fantasies might result from not being taught what is possible in reality? And what about teachers? Abandoning education in droves, quitting for reasons they can't define. Or worse: quitting without leaving the system."

He surveyed the room, reflectively shaking his head, aware even as he formed his closing words that they would be directed at himself.

"Government control over the most important years of an individual's development is a sacrifice of individual development, and the first step toward the destruction of freedom in society."

As he sped along Peninsula Drive toward the Presque Isle lighthouse, it occurred to him that he should feel uncertain about his future, or at least unemployed. Rather, he felt an exhilarating energy: the excitement of facing a new day with the means to shape it.

Three months later he traveled east in search of a suitable private school. He continued his correspondence with Rebecca, but over the next three-and-a-half years his letters became sporadic, each bearing the postmark of a different city and the brusque signature of an increasingly cynical hand.

On her fourteenth birthday he wrote:

> I am reminded by the sea of our father,
> and of things honest and resolute. I will
> return.

Word of his mother's death reached him while in Poole on his twenty-second voyage with the *Saint Sal Malone*. From London he flew to New York and Eric, only to learn that the news was four months old and that Rebecca had since been moved to the home of an aunt in Concord, New Hampshire. When he arrived there the following afternoon he found her standing before a wooden easel on the veranda, painting in the soft light of the early-autumn sun. The sight of her tears made him realize how long he had been gone, but he smiled and asked, "Why aren't you in school?"

Reluctantly, she explained that Capital City's transfer students were not permitted to enroll in Advanced Art before completing Basic Art and Art History, and that the school would allow no exceptions. Earlier that morning, she said, following an argument with a guidance counselor over her refusal to submit an assignment in the style of a famous contemporary painter, she had been dismissed from Basic Art.

Daniel studied the half-finished work on her easel, asked the name of the guidance counselor, and called a taxi. Twenty minutes later he burst unannounced through the door to Wini Minkler's office and demanded: "Who the hell do you think you are?"

The counselor took a moment to recover from her astonishment. "I beg your pardon?" she whined, peering over the rim of reading glasses from behind a massive oaken desk.

"This morning. Rebecca Nolan. Are you incapable of recognizing talent when you see it?"

"Ah . . ." she recalled. "That cute little transfer from Cleveland or somewhere. Are you her uncle? You must realize she has a very disagreeable attitude about the way art should be—"

Daniel felt a pounding in his skull and a tensing of the muscles in his abdomen when suddenly, somewhere deep inside, a restraining mechanism distorted and broke and set free a blindly savage loathing. He crossed the room and gripped the top of her desk and heaved, raising the creaking giant onto two legs as she retreated backwards in her chair. Papers, books, and a pewter stein of pens spilled onto her lap and around her feet. A drawer slid partially open, followed by another. The desk teetered for a moment, balanced on his palms, then completed its overturning with a reverberant *thud* on the carpeted floor.

His gaze rose to a silver-framed certificate on the wall behind her and a guttural sound escaped his throat. He stepped deftly onto the upended desk and slammed his fist into the center of the frame, sending shards of glass into the counselor's hair and down the open neck of her blouse.

"You are an unthinking fool," he growled at the figure cowering beneath him. "I know the importance of history and the lessons to be learned from its study, but requiring the emulation of secondhand trash as a means of teaching art is unforgivable."

He turned from her in disgust and the onlookers at the door hastened away, but a boy remained, standing in his path and staring at him with unflinching curiosity. Daniel froze, as if in startled recognition of a sight long forgotten, and the rage in his eyes gave way to a benevolent smile.

Almost tenderly he said to the boy, "Teachers who know can prove what they know. Those who cannot have nothing to teach but obedience. Reality and reason are your allies; understanding is your due."

The boy stepped aside and Daniel brushed past, but at the end of the corridor he stopped and turned and met the boy's following stare. With no trace of his earlier warmth he avowed, "It is *your* mind. Do not betray it."

III

COMMENCEMENT

EDISON

The trouble with our way of educating is that it does not give elasticity to the mind. It casts the brain into a mold. It insists that the child must accept. It does not encourage original thought or reasoning, and it lays more stress on memory than observation.

Thomas A. Edison, 1847-1931
. . . from his journals

10

SPARROW'S FLIGHT

On a cluttered cork board inside the recessed entrance to Anderson's Bookstore, fastened with a single thumbtack and illumined by an overhead lamp, a poster announced a concert the eleventh of January. It flapped and fluttered in the violent winter wind, tugging at its feeble mooring, swinging to and fro between gusts. The lamp went dark.

A few seconds later Kevin emerged, pulling shut and locking the door behind him. He raised his collar against an icy blast, and as he stepped onto the sidewalk the poster tore free. Impulsively, he grabbed for it but lost his footing, slipping and falling to the frozen pavement, clutching the rescued poster aloft in his hand. With a laugh that was half moan he returned it to the board and read for the first time the understated print at the bottom.

PHILLIP SPARROW, OPENING ACT

"Tomorrow night?" Mr. Saunders exclaimed, reaching for the television remote. "You already have plans."

Mrs. Saunders chose a magazine from the selection on the table in front of the sofa.

"Your plans, Dad," Kevin said, "not mine."

"Well, you said you'd go, and your brother's expecting you, so I think you'd better go."

"I can ride up with you some other time. You and Mom visit him almost every weekend."

Mr. Saunders fumbled with the buttons on the remote. The television's volume increased.

"Dammit," he said. "I just replaced these batteries. You said you'd go *this* weekend. Anyway, we have dinner reservations."

"I don't think it's the batteries, Ed," Mrs. Saunders suggested.

"I'm sorry," Kevin explained, "but this concert is more important to me than dinner reservations. Had I known about it earlier I wouldn't have—"

"It has to be this weekend."

"Why?"

"Because we've made arrangements."

"What arrangements?"

"I told you," he said. "Dinner."

The television channels began to change.

"With whom?"

"Dammit," Mr. Saunders repeated, slapping the remote onto the table. "Your mother and me, of course. And Edward."

"It's not the batteries, Dad," came Michelle's voice from behind the sofa.

"And?" Kevin asked.

"It's a very exclusive—"

"Mom?"

"Lou Barrett!" Mr. Saunders ceded petulantly. "The dean, all right? He and I were classmates, and I—"

Kevin silenced him with, "Have a nice reunion," and turned to leave.

"Hold it!"

Kevin stopped.

"I want the Christmas lights off the front of the house and the driveway shoveled if it snows."

"Alright."

"And I forbid you to use your mother's car."

Kevin looked back at his father and said again, "Alright."

A low-pressure front over most of the northeast produced an unseasonably mild evening. Southbound traffic into Boston was light and Kevin's bus arrived on schedule. With a brisk, unbroken stride he followed Atlantic Avenue and the surface artery from South Station to Fulton Center. Clusters of colorfully garbed youths formed a procession up the auditorium stairs—young girls beneath layers of makeup on the arms of boys bearing smuggled beer, giggling, chatting animatedly, puffing on cigarettes. Faces blended indistinguishably and most of them, Kevin realized, appeared to be in their early teens.

Ruefully, he began to wonder if anyone in the frenetic current had come to hear Phillip Sparrow, but as he traversed the second landing and glanced ahead to the entrance terrace, his misgivings, in time with his step, came to a halt.

Standing with an air of unapproachable detachment, a trim feminine figure was braced sedately against the throng, gazing over the dissonance as if oblivious to it.

Or in judgment of it, Kevin thought.

The upturned collar of her knee-length black woolen coat angled downward across her right cheekbone. The shadow under her narrow-brimmed black hat concealed her eyes. Kevin waited, motionless, fixedly watching her above the crowd, wondering what she saw or what she might be seeking. When she raised her head and the stairway lamps revealed her eyes, he realized she was looking at him.

He didn't know what made him glance away, but in the turning he wished he hadn't.

The stage appeared minuscule from Kevin's late-purchase seat, and he gazed with impatience into the girders of the orange umbrella-like ceiling. Chants summoning the featured band had risen and died many times during the past half hour; the concert should have begun twenty minutes ago. At seven-thirty-five a row of lights was extinguished, then another, parceling darkness in overlapping layers upon the crowd. The scratching of match heads and lighter flints preceded the spread of tiny yellow flames. An indistinct murmur rose from the winking void to become a demand.

"Dead End! Dead End! Dead End!" the audience shouted.

A cylinder of white light struck an empty corner of the stage, then jerked to the left and settled on a rotund bald man in a white suit stretched over a pink T-shirt.

"Whoa!" the man appealed into his microphone, breaking the chant. "Rockin' Roland here, and on behalf of W-A-V-E FM I'd like to welcome all you kids 'n' kin to one hell of a party, and you can believe me when I say it's my pleasure to be hosting tonight's show, cuz of all the concerts The Wave's brought to Boston, this one's the biggest! And I mean, B-I-G! Know why? Cuz tonight we're doing a live remote for Dead End's newest album, and you get to be a part of that album. Wadaya say about that?"

A tumultuous roar rose and fell with the DJ's fist.

"Right on!" he shouted. "I do believe you got the hang of it. Let's hear some of that when the tapes are rollin'! Okay? Okay! Now, I know everybody's anxious for the show to begin, but I'd like to say a few words about our opening act. Phillip Sparrow—"

"Dead End! Dead End! Dead—"

"Whoa! Whoa! And *whoa!*" the DJ cried. "*I* know why you're here, and *you* know why you're here, but as I started to say, the dude that's opening this show is H-O-T! And keep in mind, boys and girls, there once was a time when we never heard of Dead End either. Now, this guy brought down the house in L.A. and Detroit, so let's show him the stuff Boston's made of! How 'bout it? We're all in this together, right?"

He raised his fist and the first few rows of seats called back, "Right!"

"C'mon," he shouted. "Right?"

"*Right!*" boomed the rest of the crowd on cue.

But something wasn't right, Kevin thought, and apprehension engulfed him. The spotlight ebbed. The stage blackened.

"Ladies and gentlemen," heralded a magisterial male voice over a sepulchral rumbling rising like sludge from the floor of the hall, "please extend a warm Boston welcome to Phillip Sparrow!"

A cool bluish glow bathed the stage, illuminating five figures in white hooded robes posed statue-like at the foot of a chrome-bright ladder. A sixth, costumed from wrists to ankles in shimmering metallic silver, crouched above them on a transparent platform at the ladder's apex. Behind the frozen forms was a semicircular arrangement of musical instruments: guitars on stands, an electric piano, a tenor saxophone, an array of drums. Steadily, the rumbling became a hum and the hum an unearthly ululation. When it seemed it could grow no louder there was an explosion of dazzling light and the piercing scream of an amplified guitar. The characters at the base of the ladder threw back their hoods and cast off their robes while dashing crazily to their respective stations. The glimmering apparition above them stepped sideways into space, then floated slowly to the floor.

The beat was nervous and unfamiliar; the lyrics synthesized and scarcely intelligible. But there was no mistaking the voice of the man in silver and Kevin shuddered in recognition of the disfigured melody. He gripped the front edge of his seat as if expecting it to vanish from beneath him.

"Sparrow's Flight," he realized in a deluge of despair, might finally make the charts.

Only in his mind's periphery was he aware of standing, of forcing his way through crowded aisles, of plunging through an exit door, of fleeing across a barren granite terrace and stopping where it ended overlooking stairs that fell away to the street. For fifteen fretful minutes he stood staring through the vapor of his breath at the moon edging over Logan Airport, wishing he could have known, somehow, not to come.

"Why did you walk out?" inquired a soft voice from behind him.

He inhaled deeply and exhaled slowly. He turned. He felt blood rush to his face. It was the woman he had seen on the stairs.

"Why?" she asked again.

It took a moment for him to answer.

"That wasn't . . ." he tried. He cleared his throat. "That wasn't the Phillip Sparrow I came here to see."

She looked down at the terrace stones and nodded. Her mouth formed a knowing smile. When a moment later she looked up and approached him and said quietly, "I'm sorry," he knew she understood.

"Why did *you* walk out?" he asked.

"My curiosity was satisfied."

"Curiosity?"

She nodded. "When I heard about the concert on the radio, I remembered seeing an album cover of his, two, maybe three years ago. I wondered if his music was as good."

"Why didn't you just buy the album?"

"I didn't own a phonograph. Are you from Boston?" she asked.

"Concord."

"Massachusetts or New Hampshire?"

"New Hampshire."

"Did you drive?"

"I took the bus."

"Would you like a lift home?"

"To Concord?"

"Sure," she replied. "I'm going north. What's your name?"

"Kevin Saunders."

"Rebecca Nolan," she said, extending a gloved hand.

"What do you do?" Kevin asked as they merged into the northbound traffic on Interstate 93.

"I'm an artist," Rebecca answered. "Seven days a week I paint. Three days a week I wait tables."

"That's a ten-day week."

She gave him a smiling, sideways glance and said, "I wish it were; they come and go so quickly. What do *you* do?"

"I work in a bookstore." He hesitated. "Part time, actually. I'm still in high school."

There, he thought, he said it.

"Are you a senior?"

"Yes."

"What are your plans for next year?"

"I'm not certain. Were you when you graduated?"

"I didn't graduate."

"No?"

"I dropped out at the start of my senior year."

"Why?"

"It's a long story."

"I'm interested."

"I don't know you well enough."

He let a few seconds of silence pass and said, "If you're concerned that my response may not be worthy of an explanation, I understand. I'll ask again another time."

Her gaze remained fixed on the road, but she smiled gently and her fingers relaxed on the wheel.

"What do you think of school?" she asked.

He chuckled. "Are you sure you want to know?"

"Capital City, right? Tell me about your classes, your teachers."

"My favorite—"

"Save the best for last."

"Okay. For Economics I have Mrs. Turcotte, who has been teaching twenty-five years and who apparently believes that the most important reason for knowing anything is to pass her weekly quizzes, which are always mix-and-match, fill-in-the-blank, or multiple-choice. The key to success in her class is a photographic memory."

"That sounds familiar."

"Mrs. LeFabvre teaches Advanced Placement English. It's pretty much technical textbook stuff so it's not bad. Except for grading our tests she hardly participates, but I was in her Creative Writing class last year and every day for the first month she made us write compositions with no direction or theme, just thirty minutes of whatever 'popped'— her word—into our heads. I forget what she called it. She'd hand back our papers with a capitalized adjective scrawled across the top describing her visceral reaction to what we wrote: 'tempestuous,' 'metaphorical,' 'provocative,' et cetera. On mine she usually wrote something like, 'Relax, let it flow.'"

"Stream of consciousness," Rebecca said, stifling a laugh. "What did you write?"

"I tried to do what she asked, but short essays, mostly. I wrote my last one on the emptiness of her assignments."

Rebecca winced. "A wise choice. What did she say?"

"She was furious. She reported me to my father."

"To your *father*?"

"The principal."

"Your father's the— Oh, no!"

"He said I had no right to criticize her methods and told me to apologize or take three days detention."

"Did you apologize?"

"I wasn't sorry."

"Good. Go on."

"You're enjoying this?"

"I'm sentimental," she chortled.

"You could always go back."

"Biology."

"Mr. Theodore, *College* Biology," he emphasized sardonically. "Once a week he shows us a movie and hands out question sheets. If the class average is less than sixty percent he makes us watch it again and do the questions over."

"Earth Science."

"Mrs. Endicott. Florence 'Flo-by-the-Book' Endicott. She gives in-class reading assignments almost every day then walks out of the room with the intercom switched to *monitor*. When she returns she picks three students to orally summarize what they've read. At the end of each chapter, she copies the review questions from the back of the book and transforms them into her next test."

"Nice. Algebra."

"Last year; Mrs. Nemo. She had a thing for applying fantastically complex solutions to elementary problems. No one ever knew what she was talking about."

"Geometry."

"Sophomore year, I think. Mr. Bard, but I don't really remember his class."

"Calculus."

"I'm saving that for last."

"History."

"Left tackle."

"What?"

Kevin grinned. "Never mind, I didn't have him."

"Physics."

"A good class, originally taught by an excellent teacher until she went to work for some corporation in Nashua. I dropped it after a week with her replacement."

"Environmental Science."

"Ms. Barrymore."

"You took Environmental Science? Isn't it an elective?"

"Yes. I needed the credit, and I would not otherwise have learned that science can be validated by a majority vote, and that all life forms have equal rights."

"Did you expect objectivity?"

"No."

"Did you take Literature?"

"Modern Literature was available. Have you ever read a novel called *Beguiled!* by Edward Sherman?"

She shook her head.

"It's about twin brothers, Mark and Leo Kellogg, raised on a small farm in the Midwest. Both are in love with a girl named Eleanor, but Eleanor is ill and has only five or six years to live. Mark leaves home to study medicine so he can make Eleanor well. Leo stays on the farm to be with her. On the day when Mark finds a cure for her disease, she and Leo run away together, and Mark spends six months trying to find them. In the last few pages, when Eleanor's time is about to run out, Mark sees Leo crossing a street in Bozeman, Montana, and in his excitement runs after him and gets hit by a car and dies."

"That's it?"

"*The End.*"

"Great. Tell me about your good classes."

"Auto Shop and Calculus."

"An interesting combination."

"Mr. Sullivan teaches Auto Shop. He's thoughtful, quiet, and patient. He loves to teach what he loves to do. Mr. VanAnglin—Calculus—has no patience whatsoever. He expects his students to be like his equations: never right until perfect. He admires effort but rewards only results, and he never tolerates cheating or laziness.

"About a month ago, when the highest score on one of his tests was an eighty-five, some student's father asked at a parent-teacher meeting why he didn't scale the grades. Mr. VanAnglin's answer nearly cost him his job. I like him."

Rebecca frowned and said, "I feel sorry for him."

"You do?"

"He probably loved teaching at one time, like your Auto Shop teacher, but he's grown tired of having to struggle to do it properly. I'll bet when he started he had unlimited patience; he felt optimistic about every potential achievement and camaraderie toward fellow educators. Now, his patience is gone, he's convinced he's running out of students who want to learn, and he detests most of his associates. He won't last much longer. How old is he?"

Kevin recognized the resentment in her tone. "I hope you're wrong," he said. "I'm not sure. Late fifties."

"You like school, don't you."

The observation surprised him. "How can you tell after I've mostly been complaining about my teachers?" he asked.

"Have you ever considered teaching? As a career, I mean."

"Yes," he replied, again surprised and wondering what prompted her to inquire. "But I can't imagine—"

"I don't mean at your school, or at any school like it. I mean at a school founded on the understanding that a mind cannot be forced, that in order to learn one must *want* to learn. A school that teaches its students the value of thinking independently, with teachers who encourage and welcome the question *why*. A school with a curriculum created to inspirit self-reliant lives and where achievement is respected."

"Where is this?" he asked enthusiastically.

She shrugged.

"Oh."

Suddenly, she smiled, then looked at him and asked, "Have you ever read anything by Allesandra Wills?"

"Are you kidding?" he replied, smiling back at her. "*Spontaneous Combustion* is my favorite novel!"

"What about *An Impartial Jury*?"

"Probably my second favorite. I've read each at least three times. I wish she'd written more."

"She did."

"What?"

"A short story published in Canada under the name Sandra Willis. It's called, 'Two Days in the Life of a Dying Man.' It's different from her novels, and the writing is less polished, but I like it."

"Different in what way?"

"The protagonists in *Combustion* and *Jury* are hero types—creators, movers, extraordinary achievers. 'Two Days' is about an average man . . . sort of. His life doesn't monumentally affect or influence the world, but he honors the same values as Aris in *Combustion* and Samantha in *Jury*."

"What happens?"

She shook her head. "You'll have to read it."

"I will, but I told *you* about Mark and Leo Kellogg."

"Hardly the same," she teased.

He grinned and said, "It's up to you. You're the one who wants to tell me about it!"

"Well . . ." Her mocking smile broadened in acquiescence. "Hmm . . . Okay! It's written in two parts: 'Friday' and 'Saturday.' Are you ready?"

He nodded and settled back against the door.

"'Richard Bastion understood the measure of time. Perhaps because he knew his condition was incurable; perhaps because he knew it meant certain death. To the best of his ability he managed its symptoms, and although at times they seemed unendurable, he endured. He was thirty-eight years old.'"

"You know it verbatim?"

"Parts of it. It's nine o'clock, Friday morning. Richard is sitting behind his desk in a cluttered office at Koeppler Electronic. Across from him is Steven Doyle, the acting operations manager, and Alan Koeppler, vice president and great-grandson of the company's founder. Doyle has been called in from another plant to boost the production of a heavily marketed semiconductor line. Richard is head of the department that silver-dips, bakes, and finishes the units. He explains to Mr. Koeppler that thirty percent of the pieces he receives are improperly prepared and that Doyle has broadened their pre-dip specifications to make them officially acceptable, thereby increasing Koeppler's weekly yield. Richard, however, despite repeated warnings from Doyle, has continued to order the rejection of all un-qualified units, and his job of sixteen years is now at stake because of it."

Kevin listened ardently, as enthralled with Rebecca's attention to detail as he was by her pleasure in relating the story. Her eyes shone in the narrow strip of light cast back by the rear-view mirror, and he found himself unable to look away. When she parked in front of his house he watched her right hand, hoping she might reach for the key and switch off the ignition, but she set the brake and left the car running, tucking one leg up onto her seat and turning to face him.

"So," she resumed, "it's Saturday night. Richard reads a chapter of a book and goes to bed with his wife. Together in the dark they discuss their plans for Sunday, and she falls asleep with her hand on his chest—only to be awakened two hours later by a sudden stillness.

"The story ends with his wife composing Richard's epitaph: *As if a day was all he could have he lived eighty-one years.*"

"You mean . . . ?" Kevin began. An appreciative smile slowly crossed his face.

She returned his smile and, for the second time, gave him her hand. "I have to go," she said.

"Thank you for the ride, Rebecca. And for . . . everything."

"You're welcome, Kevin. Please call me if you ever come to Portsmouth. My number's in the book."

"Portsmouth?" he queried. "Concord wasn't on your way home."

She released the parking brake, put the car into gear, and said, "It was tonight."

Another minute passed as Kevin lay awake in bed, staring wide-eyed at the glowing green numbers on the face of his clock radio. It read twelve-fifty-seven. He noticed for the first time that the device emitted a slight hum. The empty house was otherwise silent. His mind raced.

She had asked him to call her. Well, he qualified, if he was ever in Portsmouth. But that meant she wanted to see him again, didn't it? Portsmouth wasn't far: he guessed less than fifty miles. He wasn't tired, and he had lain awake since retiring to bed at eleven.

A galvanizing resolve surged through him. He threw

aside his blanket and sheet and stood and crossed to the window. He raised the blinds. The moon was full and high; the thermometer mounted to the frame outside the glass indicated thirty-six degrees. He hurried to his dresser and pulled a sweatsuit, long underwear, and socks from its drawers and tossed them onto his bed, then went to his closet for his windbreaker, gloves, and cycling shoes.

11

SPARROW'S FLIGHT, BIS CON MOTO

Somewhere along the wooded road between Epsom and Northwood Narrows, Kevin began to doubt the rationality of his decision. It had taken an hour and a half just to travel the fifteen miles indicated by his cyclometer, and he knew that the longest, steepest hills were yet to come. The streets of Concord had been wet from melting snow, drenching his feet and lower back, but beyond the outskirts of town the untraveled pavement showed patches of ice. He grimaced at the thought of his bicycle covered with road salt and felt, as if in his ankles and knees, the grating of sand between chain and gear teeth. The headlight he had mounted to his handlebar stem brightened only a tiny patch of road a few feet ahead; twice he had been violently jarred by potholes. He could tell by the mild rhythmic pulse against his palms that one of them had put a flat spot in his front rim.

A proper repair, he knew, would have to wait, and he grew accustomed to the feeling.

At three-forty in the village of Northwood he stopped for a drink of water and part of a sandwich. He stretched for a few minutes and did jumping jacks in the middle of the road, then continued eastward. According to his calculations he was nearing the halfway point, and he pushed harder, ignoring the cold in his toes and the burn in his thighs, thinking instead of Rebecca, recalling their conversation and her voice.

He pressed a button on his cyclometer and the reading window glowed. If he could maintain this speed, he thought, he would be in Portsmouth by six.

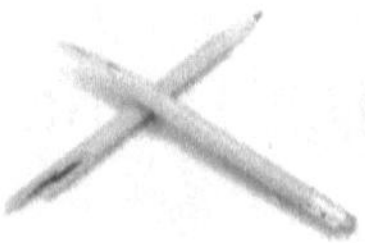

At four-fifty, a carload of drunken college students backed into the mailbox of a Durham State fraternity house. Belching and laughing, having the time of their lives finding their way by the descending moon, they coasted in neutral down Franklin Avenue to Madbury Road. The car sagged on useless suspension, weaving from lane to lane as its occupants rationed one-handed stints at the wheel. Somebody rotated a dial on the stereo to a suitable level of distortion, and with voices raised in discordant song they accelerated to beat the light at the Route 4 junction.

They didn't see the approaching cyclist swerve to avoid hitting their car. They didn't see him careen into a snowbank and strike his head against a chunk of ice. They were just kids having fun coming home from a party.

Kevin opened his eyes to the bluish smear of a streetlamp

swimming above him, unaware that he had been unconscious and that his helmet shell was fractured. The left side of his face was numb and his left arm was twisted beneath his torso. Across the road, blinking red, lay the taillight he had fastened behind his saddle. He cautiously straightened his arm and shifted his weight so he could sit, but a burning pain shot from his instep to his toes. His right foot, he could see, was still secured to the pedal. He strained to disengage the unreleased cleat, then sat upright and, with frigid hands in soggy gloves, massaged his injured ankle.

It would get him to Portsmouth, he decided.

Standing, brushing dirty snow from his chest and legs, he dragged his bicycle from the bank and stood it on the pavement. The handlebar was out of alignment with the fork and the front wheel rubbed the brake pads, but he was soon back on the road.

At five-thirty-five he crossed the northern tip of Great Bay and increased his speed under the lights of the smooth four-lane highway. There, on dry pavement, he felt his bicycle pulling slightly to the right.

He pushed on.

At five-fifty, just over the Newington-Portsmouth line, he stopped at an all-night convenience store and thumbed through a telephone directory for Rebecca's address. The book slipped from his hand when he read: *Nolan, Daniel E & Rebecca, 428 Market Street.*

At once he felt foolish and exhausted. He wandered among store aisles for several minutes before walking to where he had leaned his bicycle against the side of the building. Mechanically, he unrolled a sweater from the waterproof pannier atop his rear rack. He unbuckled and lifted off his helmet, glancing with a frown at its cracked shell. He hung it by the strap from a brake lever.

Steam rose from his back when he peeled off his windbreaker and damp sweatshirt, and he thought with vague satisfaction that at least the worst was over, but as he reached for a water bottle he noticed a ripple in the paint along the right side of his bicycle's down tube, midway between the bottom bracket and headset.

"No!" he gasped, staring in stunned disbelief at a deformation in the frame. Sick in the realization of what his rash actions had cost, drained and weak, he fell to his knees and wept.

At seven o'clock, after a breakfast of pancakes and hot chocolate at a café in Portsmouth, he telephoned Rebecca.

"Hello?" she answered in a raspy voice.

"Rebecca," he said. "this is Kevin Saunders. We met last night in—"

"Hi!" she exclaimed. "What a wonderful surprise."

"I'm glad you're home."

She laughed. "I'm still in bed."

"Oh, I'm sorry. I didn't think about the time. I'll let you get back to sleep."

"No, it's okay. My alarm should be— Hear that? Hang on a sec . . . There. Where are you?"

"Some restaurant on Maplewood Avenue."

"In Portsmouth?"

"Yes."

"That's great! Do you know how to get to Market Street?"

"I know where it is."

"Just take a left off Congress. It's an older brick town-house on the right—number four-twenty-eight."

When he didn't reply she asked, "Do you have time to stop by?"

"I . . ." He wavered. "I don't think so."

"Not even for a few minutes?"

"No one would mind?"

"Of course not!"

"What about your husband?"

"What? I'm not married."

"But . . . I saw his name listed with yours in the phone book."

"Daniel?" She laughed. "He's my brother."

With a burst of renewed energy he mounted his bicycle and pedaled through the parking lot to the street. His ankle was painfully swollen, but nine minutes later he was standing at the threshold of his destination. He knocked at the weathered wooden door. It opened.

"Good morning," he said. "I'm sorry to be calling so . . ." He fell silent, staring into the dark-gold eyes of the shirtless bearded man standing before him. Several seconds passed. When the man prompted brusquely, "Well?" all Kevin could manage in reply was a single astounded sentence rendered as a whisper.

"I know you!"

12

THE TEACHER

Daniel turned and walked back into the house.

"It was three years ago," Kevin recounted, following him through the open door into a narrow unlighted hallway. "At Capital City High School in Concord. I know it was you."

Daniel emerged from the kitchen with a mug of coffee and started up the stairs at the end of the hall. Without pausing or looking back he said, "If Rebecca is expecting you I'm sure she'll be down. Close the door."

"Outside the guidance office," Kevin called after him. "You said, 'It's your mind. Don't betray it.'"

Daniel stopped, then turned.

"What else?" he asked.

"Teachers who know can prove what they know. Those who cannot have nothing to teach but obedience. Reality—"

"And you memorized it like a good little student?"

Kevin stared undaunted into Daniel's cold gaze and said, "At first."

"At first?"

"Yes. Then I learned it."

"Close the door," Daniel repeated impassively, disappearing up the stairs before Kevin could speak again. A minute later, Rebecca came down.

"Good morning," she said, smiling and barefoot in an oversized ivory T-shirt tucked into unbelted jeans. She held long black socks in her left hand and short black boots in her right. The casual indifference of her attire stressed an unpremeditated sensuality.

"Good morning," Kevin replied. He pointed past her up the stairs. "I know him."

"You know . . . Daniel?"

"He came to my high school."

"What would—" She paused, remembering the day, and Kevin detected a gleam of interest in her eyes. In an instant it vanished.

"What happened to your clothes?" she asked.

He scrutinized his salt-stained sweatpants. "The roads were wet," he replied.

"What did you do?" she prodded with a quizzical laugh. "Walk?"

"No . . . I rode my bicycle."

"From Concord?"

He nodded.

"All night? In the middle of winter?"

He nodded again. "Could we sit?"

He left his shoes by the door and walked with her into the living room. He tried not to favor his ankle, but she noticed and asked with concern, "Will you be alright?"

"Yes," he answered, "but I ruined my bicycle."

She motioned for him to join her on the sofa. "I'm sorry," she said, "but, Kevin, why would you attempt such a thing? You could have been seriously hurt."

"I know."

She faced him and queried, "You know?"

"I couldn't stop thinking about you," he admitted hastily.

"When you called I got the impression you weren't sure you wanted to see me."

"I thought you were married."

"Yet, still, you called."

"Yes."

"Well . . . I'm glad you did. Have you eaten?"

"At the restaurant. Could I please use your shower?"

"Of course. The bathroom is at the top of the stairs. You'll find towels in the closet to the left of the door, and there'll be pants and a shirt hanging on the doorknob by the time you're finished. I think Daniel's will fit you well enough."

"What does he do?"

She bent forward and pulled one sock over her left foot, then the other over her right. "He's a deckhand," she answered, straightening, "on a freighter."

"Why was he at my high school?"

"It was my high school, too, for about a month."

"You went to Capital City?"

"Three years ago."

"And then dropped out?"

"Yes. Daniel brought me here to Portsmouth. He rented this house. He spent the next five months as my tutor."

"Where were your— What do you mean, your *tutor*?"

"He was a teacher. Before."

"What did he teach? Where?"

She smiled unhappily, wriggling her left foot into the top of a boot. It slipped away from her on the hardwood floor. She kicked the other boot after it.

"History," she said. "He started at a public high school

in Erie, Pennsylvania, then drifted for a while between private schools. He taught at several and quit within a few months each time."

"What happened?"

"It's what *didn't* happen. He went to those schools knowing—"

She stopped mid-sentence, looking past Kevin toward the hall. He followed her gaze to find Daniel standing in the doorway.

"I remember you," Daniel remarked introspectively, buttoning a khaki canvas shirt. "At least, I remember the impertinent, inquisitive bravado in the eyes of a boy. What is your name?"

"Kevin Saunders."

Daniel entered the room and walked past them, stopping before the French windows at the balcony. When he turned his head partway in their direction, the white sky softened his sculpted visage.

"I almost knocked you down, Kevin Saunders," he commented in recollection. "But you never even blinked and I thought, 'They haven't reached this one yet. They haven't stamped their seal of approval on his brain.'"

He exhaled. He turned to fully face them before continuing.

"I spoke to you because it seemed there might be a chance for your mind to survive their system. I apologize for my rudeness just now. You asked Rebecca why I quit teaching? Ask first, what is required of learning? What is the purpose of education? What social, political, and economic conditions presuppose the existence of a proper educational system? Contrast the answers to those questions with the concept of public schooling, and you'll see the reason for the distance between what education should be and what it has become."

"What should it be?" Kevin asked. He did not look at Rebecca, but he felt a tension in her posture that had not existed a moment earlier, and although she still sat close to him on the sofa he felt as if she had moved away.

"Education belongs on the free market—not under the thumb of government—and until parents understand that, their children will be marched one generation at a time toward a day when individual thought is a relic and individual rights have been erased from history."

"You mean—" Kevin began.

"I mean it is immoral for a government to force its citizens to attend school, whether by majority vote or totalitarian decree, and it is immoral for a government to tax its citizens for the funding of their neighbor's children's coerced education. Our public-school system represents the most meaningful step toward statism this country has ever taken. *Think about it.* It claims the authority to forcibly remove children from their homes for the purpose of subjecting their unformed minds to a daily decade-long barrage of government-prescribed training—with or without the consent of their parents. It claims the authority to extort payment from its citizens for the training of these children as if they were *everyone's* children.

"State-controlled learning is grotesquely incompatible with a country created in the name of freedom and individual rights, and Americans are guilty *en masse* of ignorance or apathy. Those who truly think that the earnings of all should be forcibly taken for the education of some—or even more absurdly that government knows best what to teach a child—should relocate to a country created to be authoritarian instead of helping to destroy this one."

"People believe they have a right to an education," Kevin said, "because it's so important."

"There is no such thing as a *right* to violate another person's rights, which is essential to the means of achieving public education's ends. The right to a *thing*—whether product, service, or resource—contradicts the definition of rights. There is only the right to be free to produce or earn that product, service, or resource, no matter how important some authority—or the public—deems it."

"What about private schools?" Kevin asked.

"Except for the details of funding, there are no private schools. Nothing is private that is forbidden to exist without government permission and oversight. Most so-called private schools are church affiliated, and their nonpublic nature derives more from religious than educational doctrine, though they consider the two inseparable. Their standards are very often higher than those of public schools, leaving aside the notion that biblical dogma is the wellspring of knowledge. The so-called progressive private schools, well . . ." He paused. "I taught briefly at several and observed primarily a veneer of respectability. The facilities and grounds were better kept and there was a general air of intellectualism, but modern educational theory nonetheless prevailed, which is to say, students were not being taught to think."

He approached them and sat on the arm of a much-used brown-leather chair across from the sofa. "Why do you remember what I told you that day?" he asked.

"I suppose because I *heard* you, and because what you said seemed self-evident."

"You mean, it felt right?"

"No. I mean it seemed—it *is*—self-evident."

"Explain."

"Teachers who know," Kevin answered, "can prove what they know by referencing reality and—"

"Which reality?"

"What do you mean *which* reality?"

"Millions of people believe in more than one."

"And their beliefs are based on ... what? Faith in someone else's beliefs? Wishful thinking? We can believe in Santa Claus but unless we can point to him in reality or validate his existence logically, we can't *know* that there is a Santa Claus."

"What about those who denounce proof? Might they possess a 'higher' intelligence, as they'd have us believe?"

"No. To deny the evidence of one's senses, to reject proof in favor of the unprovable, is to give up your mind. To betray your mind."

There was a smile in Daniel's eyes when he spoke again. "How is it that you—"

His words were severed when Rebecca stood and abruptly exited the room. Kevin turned, perplexed. He caught up with her in the hall.

"What's wrong?" he asked.

"Forget it," she answered sharply, grabbing her coat and purse from a closet under the stairs and stepping into a pair of unzipped winter boots.

"Where are you going?"

"Out," she said. She plucked a hat from a hanger then walked to the front door and yanked it open and left it ajar behind her. He followed in stocking feet along a slushy path that ended at a wood-framed carport.

"Rebecca?" he implored.

She stopped beside her car and searched her purse. She withdrew a cluster of keys.

"I don't know what—" he said.

"Forget it."

He watched her back the car into the street and drive away. He returned to an empty living room.

"Kevin?" called Mrs. Saunders from the bottom of the stairs. "We're home."

"Kevin?" echoed Michelle. "We're home."

"Go and see if he's in his room."

Michelle scrambled noisily up he stairs. "Nope," she hollered, "and he didn't make his bed."

Mrs. Saunders hung her handbag from the back of a dining chair and stood looking about the room while peeling off a leather glove one finger at a time. Mr. Saunders walked through into the kitchen carrying a suitcase and two plastic sacks of groceries.

"At least the car's still here," he grumbled. "Michelle!" he shouted back toward the stairs, but she peeked around the corner from the dining room. "Oh," he said. "Go see if his bike's in the basement."

Under his breath he conceded, "He got the Christmas lights down."

A telephone in the house rang eleven times.

Kevin stood on the first-floor balcony with his palms on the stained-wood railing, staring into the gray-green water of the Piscataqua as it roiled and churned with the incoming tide. Beneath him, in the mud at the river's edge, two brown herring gulls rummaged for breakfast through a tear in a white garbage bag. A tern, smaller and gray with a blood-red bill, landed between them only to be hailed by a volley of agitated squawks and wing flapping. Unimpressed, it hopped nonchalantly aside while the gulls went back to their project. When one of them extracted a crust of bread, the waiting tern aptly snatched it away and vanished upriver.

"Dumb birds," Kevin complained restlessly. The telephone beckoned again and he went inside to answer it.

"Nolan residence," he said after the sixth ring.

"Kevin? It's Rebecca. I was afraid you might have left. I called a few minutes ago but there was no answer."

"I was outside. I thought Daniel would get it."

"Kevin," she said, "I'm sorry I walked out on you, it's just that he and I used to be so close, and for the last couple of years he's drifted further and further away. I suppose I felt a little jealous, seeing him speak with a stranger as if I wasn't even there."

"Thank you for telling me."

"Will you accept my apology?"

"Of course. Where are you?"

"Wallis Sands. I was thinking, if you have time I'd like to take you to see one of my paintings."

"I'd enjoy that. The bus to Concord doesn't leave until three."

"Great. Put your bicycle on the balcony. I'll be back in twenty minutes."

He disconnected and turned to find Daniel standing by the sofa wearing a white open-necked shirt and jeans that looked new. He was clean shaven.

"Are you going home today?" he asked.

"I have school in the morning."

"Skip it."

"Why?"

"I have work to do this afternoon, but I thought we

might talk again tomorrow. Maybe drive out to Jenness Beach if the weather's good."

"I'll ask Rebecca."

"Fine. The three of us, of course." After a thoughtful pause, he asked, "She's okay, isn't she?"

"I think so."

"I didn't mean to . . . I should have realized—"

"May I ask you a question?"

"Certainly."

"I think I understand what you were saying about education and the government, and I think I understand how hard it must be knowing that the only place you can teach is in a system you disdain, but I wonder if it wouldn't be worth fighting to make it right. Even if you tried a hundred schools, or started your own, or tutored privately, I think it would be worthwhile trying to achieve in the future what you would like to have now."

"What's your question?"

"Are you a teacher? Or a deckhand?"

Daniel nodded slowly, then smiled without emotion and replied, "I am a teacher."

The painting hung alone in a lighted shallow cove at the rear of Schernthaner's Gallery in Exeter. Below it, engraved into a brass plate, was the title *Two Windows*. Occupying the left half of the broad canvas was one window closed and latched, it's casement frame rough with flakes of peeling white paint. Fingered in the film of a dusty pane was a stick-figure man with a round blank face. Beyond lay a desolate expanse of cracked bleached earth, a hopeless, lifeless wasteland. A second window filled the right half of the canvas. It was identical to the first but open, with an unblemished finish. Through its clean clear panes could be seen in the distance a towering silver-blue city. The canvas was signed in the lower-right corner, *RWN*.

As Kevin stood in admiration of her work, Rebecca watched from across the room. Her gaze traced the line of his legs, his hips and waist, his back and shoulders. Their eyes met when he turned to face her.

"I suspect Daniel thinks I earn my living as an artist," she said outside the car. "I do okay, but I'm not sure he knows I need my other job."

"Do you enjoy it?"

"The hours and pay are good, but some of the customers . . ." She displayed an amused smile as she unlocked and opened the passenger door.

"What about some of the customers?" Kevin asked.

"Well," she said, circling the front of the car and sliding in behind the steering wheel. She closed her door. "Rather than ask how a particular dish is prepared, customers I've never met want to know if they, personally, will like it. 'Which do you think I'd prefer,' they ask, 'the New York sirloin or your filet-of-sole Florentine?'"

"Oh," Kevin said. "How do you answer *that*?"

"Usually I just tell them what is popular, which seems to be what they want to hear—though it's not always what I'd like to tell them. I waited on a party of six the other night and the first man asked for a cocktail, but when he realized no one else was drinking he canceled his order.

Then, while I was at another table, his wife called me back to say she'd changed her mind, and so had her husband. When I brought their drinks, everybody wanted one."

She started the car and turned a knob for the heater fan, then slid a lever to *defrost*.

"There's the man sitting behind an empty plate who wants to argue that his steak was overcooked, and the women who gab for twenty minutes after being served then complain that their food is cold. And the couple who boast of their friendship with the owner while asking if I could please send her to their table before bringing the bill. And the double-daters who wonder at six-thirty if they can make it to a seven o'clock movie without being rushed. And the occasional disappearing salt-and-pepper shakers and silverware and table rose. Of course we have good customers, too, but I'd rather spend all of my time painting. Being confident that I can eventually do that makes waitressing tolerable."

She looked at Kevin and asked, "Could you stay another day? Daniel wants us to go with him to Jenness Beach in the morning."

"I told him I'd ask you."

"Then it's settled." She checked the rear-view and side mirrors and put the car into gear and said, "Daniel's clothes fit you well."

That night, while her guest lay sleeping on the sofa downstairs, Rebecca faced the floor-standing mirror in the corner beside her bed. A contrary lock of her towel-dried hair fell in a glistening black line over her left eye and cheek. A droplet of bathwater trickled downward from her temple past the corner of her mouth. She untied her robe and shrugged it from her shoulders and let it slip to the floor, recalling Kevin's gaze upon her painting. She turned slightly, clasping her hands behind her neck, stretching, extending, elongating the taper of her waist and accentuating the arch of her lower back, abstracting from her reflection a living self-portrait.

She brought her right hand forward and trailed her fingers in brush-like strokes across her skin, along her jaw and lips to the hollow at the base of her throat, above her collarbone and left shoulder to the underside of that uplifted arm, beneath the corrugation of her ribs and over the gentle incline of her breasts, following in descent the inverted slope of her abdomen, shading, blending, transposing, lingering, until desire overwhelmed her portrait's theme.

She collapsed across her bed under an oval of light projected by the lamp on her nightstand, basking in a montage of luxuriant color.

13

A CONCEPTUAL EDUCATION

At nine-fifteen Monday morning, Mr. Saunders was informed that his school was one of twelve chosen for Phase One of the New American People's Educational System. The congratulatory call from Washington came unexpectedly, and he wasn't sure what to think until he told Dr. Minkler, who seemed to have been expecting it.

"Of course it's an honor," she gushed assuredly. "Do you know how many public schools there are in this country? Imagine, to be one of only twelve! You should be proud: of your staff, your students, yourself, your school. *Your* school!"

Dr. Minkler had been appointed Regional Director of Community Relations, but this was no surprise to her either. All she had needed was confirmation of Secretary Winfield's visit to the school. She canceled her appointments and locked her office door and began preparations for a Friday assembly.

Down the corridor, Dana Brissette leaned against the wall beside the door to Mr. Sullivan's office. The fingers of his left hand drummed the cover of a book in the stack pinned lopsidedly between his right hip and arm. His eyes were bloodshot. Mr. Sullivan closed a file-cabinet drawer and called him in.

"What can I do for you, Dana?" he asked.

"Well, Kevin Saunders and I have Ms. Barrymore for Environmental Studies, but he's not in class, and I was wondering whether or not you've seen him today."

"No, I haven't. In fact, I think I saw his name on the absentee—" His eyes narrowed. "Are you okay?"

"Yes, sir. I just needed to talk with Kevin. I guess I'll go back to class." His voice trembled and he shifted his hold on his books but made no motion to leave.

"Here," said Mr. Sullivan, reaching to help. "Why don't you put these down and talk to me."

"I'm okay," Dana insisted, relinquishing the books. "It's just, well, we were discussing Selective Service in my U.S. Government class last period, and Coach Brandt asked if anyone thought it was wrong. I turn eighteen tomorrow and I've been thinking about it, and I raised my hand. Most of the girls raised their hands, too, but I don't think any of the other boys did, and all of a sudden he started teasing me. He wouldn't even let me say why I thought it was wrong, he just—"

His lower lip quivered and he pushed his hands into his pockets. He looked down at Mr. Sullivan's desk.

"He asked if I was afraid to serve my country, but I wasn't sure how to answer that kind of question and when I told him I thought the draft was unconstitutional he became sarcastic. He said it wasn't. Unconstitutional, I mean. He said guys like me just use that as an excuse and that if we were gun shy we should join the women's army. He said I was the only boy out of all his classes—"

"Mr. Sullivan?" crackled a voice over the intercom.

"Thanks anyway," said Dana retreating through the

door and across the classroom into the corridor, leaving his books where Mr. Sullivan had placed them on his desk.

Kevin awakened to the smell of coffee, his legs stiff and his ankle sore. On a coaster on the table by the sofa was a tall glass of orange juice. He sat up and reached for it.

"Good morning," Rebecca called from the kitchen. "What would you like in your omelet? Peppers? Mushrooms? Onions? Cheese?"

"What?" he asked groggily, turning toward her voice.

"Peppers, mushrooms, and cheese," she answered for him. "Do you drink coffee?"

"Coffee . . ." he repeated. He stared at his orange juice.

She laughed, entering the room with a steaming mug and setting it on a second coaster. "I guessed cream, no sugar," she said. "Did you get enough sleep?"

He nodded. "You?"

"I've been up since seven."

"Where's Daniel?"

"I think he just got out of the shower. Drink up and get dressed. Breakfast is almost ready."

At ten they drove to Straw's Point in Rye. Rebecca parked at the end of Locke Road, and they followed a rutted path over the storm wall to the rocky beach. The sun warmed their faces as they walked, and with the temperature approaching forty degrees it felt like spring. After a hundred or so yards of silence, Daniel said: "I pledge allegiance to the flag of the United States of America, and to the republic for which it stands, one nation, under God, indivisible, with liberty and justice for all."

Kevin glanced at him, curious. Rebecca grinned.

"I recited that proclamation every morning in home-room from first through ninth grade," Daniel elucidated. "I was never told why, its meaning was never explained, and it never occurred to me that I should ask. But one day early in my sophomore year, a boy named Jason refused to stand with the class and was sent to the principal's office. He refused again the next day and was told to lead the pledge for a week or stay for detention. He chose deten-tion, and this went on until his parents and the principal reached an agreement: Jason would be excused from recit-ing the pledge provided he stood, hand over heart, while everyone else spoke it.

"This boy had a well-deserved reputation as a trouble-maker, and I knew he intended rebellion as an end in it-self, but it was the school's response to his behavior that made me realize how easily one can become unthinkingly caught up in commonplace rituals. If one does not under-stand and endorse a daily vow of political allegiance, one has nothing to gain by mouthing the words, so to whom or to what does its value, if any, go?

"That incident greatly affected my eventual regard for education. You see, soon after Jason's behavior ceased to be an issue, I asked every teacher at Irving High: 'Why do we begin each day with an oath to national duty, and what bearing does such an oath have on the things we're here to learn?' You can imagine the sort of answers I received. The best was a thoughtful, 'I'm not sure,' and I knew that was not good enough."

"Did you stop saying it?" Kevin asked.

"I rewrote it as a pledge of appreciation: I see my freedom in the flag of the United States of America, and in the founding ideals for which it must stand, one nation, built by men, irrepressible, with liberty and justice for each."

He laughed in recollection and commented, "Less than perfect, perhaps, but not bad for a fifteen-year-old."

The point's narrow expanse of wave-worn rock gave way to the tractable soft sand of Jenness Beach. Kevin wished he had wrapped his ankle. Annoyed, he put the pain from his mind and tried not to limp as Daniel continued.

"I persisted in asking such questions and discovered that too few teachers could sensibly explain the purpose of their subjects in practical application to life after school—and I don't mean vocational classes or sex education or home economics or personal hygiene, but the four subjects that form the basis of a proper education.

"Do you know what is the purpose and value of being a proficient writer?"

"To communicate accurately?" Kevin replied, not intending his words to sound like a question.

"Writing teaches the brain to be proficient at thinking. It is a tool to establish and perfect structure in an otherwise informal procession of thought. Writing provides the thinker with an opportunity to make visual contact with the contents of his mind, and to then subject that content to analysis from innumerable perspectives. Writing is, in fact, the only way for an individual to organize and clarify thoughts relevant to complex subjects, and rewriting is the process of making those thoughts better and better. Writing is to the conceptual faculty a boundless multidimensional mirror, and a prerequisite to the understanding of logical thought. The student who knows how to write will know how to think, and at the outset he must learn that words have exact meanings, because inexact words represent inexact thought—a precondition to the mistaken view that there are no absolutes, which is itself an absolute, and that life is unknowable.

"I had an English teacher who offered extra credit for essays written in other classes. In my school, assignments and exams would be given in essay form, except for mathematics, and students would be graded on both the correctness of their answers and the quality of their writing.

"In other words, every teacher would teach writing—meaning every teacher would have to know how to think. The language itself—spelling, grammar, punctuation, the fundamentals of form and composition—would be taught early in a child's education. Properly presented, classes in English would be necessary only through sixth or seventh grade, and the first words the child would read would be those he had written."

"Why his own writing?" Rebecca asked.

Kevin glanced at her walking in the damp sand a few paces downslope from Daniel. She was carrying the pale-green sweater she had worn in the car, and had rolled the cuffs of her darker-green linen pants over her calves.

"Because reading and writing are inseparable, except through today's education, and since the mind of greatest consequence to a student's life is his own, the most important thing to read is his own writing. Beyond that, reading opens the door to all things conceptual. It is the passkey to the realm of ideas and to the sum of human knowledge, and it makes intimately accessible a lifetime of learning, adventure, and inspiration—which is part of the reason I advocate the teaching of world literature as an essential.

"You see, the art of literature provides a view of life in the framed form of another mind's concepts. It teaches how other men might think and act; it shows places and times we might not otherwise experience; it can broaden a reader's picture of his own life through a comparison of characters; it can illustrate the world as it used to be, as it is, as it might be, as it should be. And it can teach values without dictating values. Properly taught, literature can serve as an integrator of every other subject.

"Do you know what is the purpose and value of teaching mathematics?" he asked with scarcely a pause.

"Wait," Kevin intervened. "You said, *world* literature. Why wor—"

"The literature of isolated cultures gives us culturally isolated perspectives, just as the literature of an isolated period provides only a fractional-time perspective. There is nothing wrong with the specialized study of literature from specific cultures and periods, but knowing the larger context within which these ideas and expressions and languages exist is fundamental, and it is necessary to distinguish *education*—the teaching of life-critical fundamentals—from career training.

"Despite the way they are presented, the two are not interchangeable. Education is the groundwork, foundation, and frame—the core structure—for career training. From that structure, career interests can be explored and choices developed. Do you understand?"

Kevin nodded.

"You're describing a building," Rebecca said. "You're saying that the third floor can't be built before the first, and that the first floor will only stand if the foundation is good."

"Certainly. Every building—whether one story or a hundred—begins with and forever rests upon its foundation. And the strength and longevity of the structure above its foundation relies upon the integrity of its frame. In education, that means developing the essential tool for choosing and building the structure of a life. Education creates the foundation and frame. Training, by contrast, develops systems and components complementary to the building's purpose."

"And mathematics?" Kevin asked.

"Do you know the consequence of *not* knowing the purpose and value of teaching mathematics? I've seen entire classes hopelessly buried beneath piles of abstractions when all that was needed to prevent a garden of logic from becoming a wilderness of gibberish was a teacher who understood application.

"It is through the proper teaching of mathematics that students can learn the elements of logic, the essence of the conceptual process. Students must be shown what has been made knowable and possible to man via mathematics. They must learn it as the science that brings the universe into a comprehensible perspective, in the same reality-tied way they learned that three apples from five equals two. They should emerge from class knowing the functionality of logic, knowing how percepts relate to concepts and how concepts relate to higher concepts. They should consistently be given real-life examples, not forgettable tangles of seemingly useless equations.

"Knowledge is not an end in itself. It is practical, and its practicality must be illustrated with every lesson in every subject. Anything less is a corruption of the educational process and the beginning of the end of knowledge."

"Most of my science classes were taught that way," said Kevin.

"I'm sure they were, but the purpose of science class is to provide students with useful knowledge about the physical world that is their home. Scientific method is important, but not primary, and specialization is superfluous unless teaching future scientists in college. It's one thing to teach the rudiments of mineral testing in order to explain earth's physical composition, but students trapped in a lab testing minerals will discover only boredom, resulting in a foggy notion that geology has something to do with scraping rocks together and weighing them underwater.

"Science must teach the laws of nature and the nature of reality. A teacher cannot expect students to understand theories and formulations when no reason or motivation is provided to encourage understanding. We live in a cause-and-effect universe, a knowable universe, and it is the science teacher's job to turn out young men and women who understand the principles that make it so.

"Kevin, I was twelve when I decided to be a teacher; I was fourteen when I chose history as the subject I would teach. That any child would want to pursue what is typically the least inspiring of all classes might seem strange, but I was fascinated by time as a concept and man's relationship with it.

"History is the all-inclusive educational subject. Every act becomes, once performed, history. When taught as the systematic study of human life through past interactions, it provides a factual base from which every other subject can be presented. When taught as a hodgepodge of names and dates, as is standard today, it disintegrates to the status of a trivia game played for credit."

Kevin laughed.

"What?" Daniel asked.

"Sorry," Kevin replied. "Nothing."

"The inattentively repeated adage, 'history repeats itself,' deserves focused attention. Men repeat the actions of other men across cultures and time, sometimes by intention, sometimes by omission. History gives us the opportunity to review and evaluate human causal principles, and with this insight better direct our future. There is so much to learn about man's nature and potential by understanding his achievements and failures, and one of the most destructive betrayals of modern education is its failure to teach history objectively.

"And that's it," Daniel concluded, angling toward his sister and placing his arm over her shoulder. "The essential curriculum for a conceptual education: literature, mathematics, science, and history—with writing taught throughout. A serious, categorically defined, long-range program of systematic, motivated, logical, reality-oriented study in priority subjects. Not child care and family planning, or auto mechanics and metal trades, or agriculture and secretarial science, or French or chorus or crafts or parallel parking, because *time is limited*. And when home economics is taught on a par with science it will be on a common level that students perceive both, which makes a parody of values."

"Home Ec and subjects like that earn fewer credits, I think," Kevin proposed.

"A sensible gesture," Daniel acknowledged, "but such subjects do not belong in a program of education. If there is time at the end of the day for workshops in band or typing or whatever, fine, but only after the essentials for life as an adult have been learned."

"One of my best-taught classes is Auto Shop," Kevin said, smiling at the image of a bespectacled gentleman standing beside a chalkboard on wheels.

"That may be, but learning how to repair a car is infinitely less important than learning how to use your mind. Anyone who wants to be a good mechanic must first learn how to think."

"But every student in my Auto Shop class takes it seriously. More seriously than their other classes, I'd say."

"Why do you suppose that is?"

"Because they respect the teacher."

"Because they know *why* they are taking the class. Auto Shop matters because it means something to their lives and futures. Does the teacher know his subject?"

"Yes."

"Does he love his subject?"

"Definitely."

"Does he know how to communicate it?"

"Yes."

"Does he make it make sense?"

"Yes."

"Then students who can apply to their thinking what they learn from this teacher about car repair will have learned something more useful than car repair." He turned toward Kevin and added, "That list, by the way, which you answered in the affirmative, is why students respect your Auto Shop teacher."

"What about art?" asked Rebecca.

Daniel pulled his sister closer as they walked.

"You know my regard for the importance of art," he said, "but painting, sculpture, theater, music, and dance do not belong in a basic curriculum except when presented in history class as cultural representations of various periods. The art that should be taught is literature because it is expressed and interpreted conceptually.

"Keep in mind I am *not* prescribing seven burdensome hours of intellectual expenditure. I'm talking about a few critical subjects given as the foundation on which to build life as a thinking human being. Classes in other subjects as a break from that central conceptual theme are optional."

"What about philosophy, politics, and psychology?" Kevin asked.

"Philosophical abstractions are too advanced for children to apply to reality, though the basics could be offered transitionally during a student's final year of schooling. Implicitly, philosophy can be explored through the study of literature. As for political science, children are incapable of making adult conceptualizations, so the only way to teach politics is through the delivery of unanchored data. Correspondingly, as a direct result of their inadequate education, I would guess that half of America's adult population engages in politics at a child's conceptual level.

"Psychology? It's too specialized. Students should be aware of its existence and purpose—along with paleontology, archaeology, herpetology, entomology, and so on—but beyond a cursory introduction it's a course to be studied in college."

"What about college?" Rebecca asked at the same time Kevin said, "What about religion?"

"Colleges mirror the system that supplies them, and since they reinject that system with teachers, a cycle of self-perpetuating educational deterioration is guaranteed. Even if that weren't true, advanced subjects are a waste without the foundation I've described, and college is not the place to learn what a system of education failed to teach. With few exceptions, it's too late. College should be for specialized training after education."

"Then you think going to college can be a good thing?" Kevin asked.

"Sure. It depends on the requirements of one's field and how it's taught. A college degree, and what that presumably represents, can be of value to a variety of professions, but students have to determine its value according to the standards of their intended careers. There's no such thing as a college education, however. Education comes before college.

"Religion, like philosophy, should be presented within the study of history and literature, and in the same manner—as opposed to an indoctrination. Moral choices and consequences are observable all around us every day, but moral *teachings* belong in the home, not in school.

"Yesterday you told me," he said to Kevin, "'People believe they have a right to an education.'"

"Not all people, obviously," Kevin responded, "but don't you think it's taken for granted that attending first through twelfth grade is an automatic part of life?"

"Absolutely. Failing to question what everyone does usually results in automatic participation."

"And since primary education is imposed by law and people are taxed for it anyway—"

"They have even less reason to think about it and more reason to consider it their due."

"That's what I meant. Even if people weren't taxed to pay for public schools, if they had to choose their schools and pay for them personally, they'd feel like a necessity had been taken from them."

"I understand. Consider another necessary product as a right, imagine hearing this as a presidential decree." He raised his voice slightly. "My fellow Americans, automobiles are no longer a convenience, they are an integral part of our daily lives. We need them. We drive to work, to school, to the store, to the movies, to the airport, to the doctor's office. Most of us take such freedom for granted, owning two or three cars, never realizing there are many less fortunate who can barely afford even one. Through no fault of their own, millions of Americans drive dangerous wrecks with bald tires, defective brakes, broken headlights, shredded upholstery—while the rich tool around in decadent luxury. It's a documented fact that countless ordinary citizens risk breakdown each day just because they can't make the payments on a decent car.

"Well, no one—regardless of income, race, religion, or sex—will ever have to face that inequity again, because we have just signed into law . . ." Daniel delayed, smiling, and announced, "*The Open Road Act.*

"We have appointed staff at the federal level, that will appoint staff at the state level, that will direct officials at the community level in the determination of vehicular need. As a rule, a family of four will be assigned two cars, but each case will be decided on its own merit based on the findings of local officials. Every five years thereafter cars will be replaced or repaired according to the discretion of the community board. Naturally we'll see a slight tax increase, and model selection could be somewhat limited, but transportation security on a national scale outweighs such trivialities. For decades we've boasted the finest highway system in the world. Now, at last, everyone can share in its benefits."

He grinned at Kevin's skeptically standoffish expression. "Of course," he imparted quietly, "when that failed, as it would despite backroom deals with auto manufacturers and oil producers, the next step would be the elimination of all privately owned motor vehicles in lieu of mandatory public transportation. The point, however, is that if such a program had been in effect for the last eighty years, replacing it with a self-sustaining, self-correcting, choice-based market would seem as absurd to most people as the separation of government and education—or medicine, retirement, banking, and so on."

Daniel stopped. He stared at Kevin disapprovingly.

"You shouldn't be walking on that ankle," he chastened. He pointed to a huge oblong boulder perched on the top of a concrete storm wall, two hundred yards down the beach. "That's where Perkins Road ends. I'll meet you there with the car in twenty minutes."

With a wink at Rebecca as she handed him her keys he said, "So much for the fiddle player!"

Kevin watched Daniel jog back toward Straw's Point,

then asked, "What did he mean by that?"

"Oh," she sighed, resuming their walk, "it's just an expression. You know, the one about paying the fiddler."

He thought he saw a blush in her cheeks; after a moment he looked away. He bent mid-stride, scooped up a polished flat stone, and threw it sidearm into the waves.

"The other night," he said, kneeling to select another, "when I saw you on the steps to the concert hall . . ."

"Yes?"

He stood and sent the second stone skimming after the first. He told her, "I don't know why I looked away."

She smiled and took his hand, and they progressed in silence to the break in the storm wall at Perkins Road.

And then he was home, sitting at his desk, staring at the notes he had left there Saturday. He felt as if he had been roused from a dream; the last two days seemed such a contrast. He realized with dismay that he dreaded returning to school.

He leaned back in his chair and gazed meditatively at the painting on the wall above his desk, at the precious flecks of cascading hourglass gold, at the conflicting waves, at the trio of initials signed in the lower-right corner.

14

EXTRAPOLATION

*T*uesday's absentee report lay among the scattered papers on Mr. Sullivan's desk. Dana Brissette headed the grade-twelve list.

"I'm concerned, Kevin," said Mr. Sullivan, tapping the list with his pen. "I don't think he's missed a day of school since eighth grade."

"What did his mother say when you called?"

Mr. Sullivan had summarized what Dana told him yesterday. To that he contributed, "Only that Dana had a disagreement with a teacher, and that his father had taken the teacher's side."

Kevin set his books beside Dana's on the file cabinet and started out the door.

"Where are you going?" Mr. Sullivan asked.

"Down the hall. I'll be back in a few minutes."

There was wrath in Kevin's step as he rounded the corner and climbed the stairs, but by the time he reached room 207 all he felt was an impersonal sense of commitment. He opened the door without knocking and walked in.

Desks were clumped together in groups of three and four; boys were perched on the backs of chairs in a huddle at the front of the room. Only a few students appeared to be studying. Kevin pushed the door closed behind him.

"What do *you* want?" Brandt drawled, looking up from the huddle.

Heads turned and some of the murmur subsided, but when Kevin replied in the tone of a command, "Repeat to me what you said yesterday to Dana Brissette," a foreboding hush rippled across the room.

Brandt laughed contemptuously and said, "Get the hell out of my class."

"Class?" Kevin countered. "This isn't a class. It's a scheduled waste of time. I'm not leaving until someone tells me what happened."

"Why you ... you insolent son of a bitch," Brandt rumbled. "You'll leave when I tell you to leave! And no one here has anythin' to say, either," he tacked on, standing and glaring menacingly over the heads of his students.

There was a self-assured calmness about Kevin's demeanor, a sense of certainty in confrontation that he had never before experienced. He gestured with one hand at Brandt's students.

"They wouldn't be afraid of you if they knew you," he said evenly, "if they realized that it's only their unfocused thinking that makes someone like you possible. You subjected a thoughtful young man to your half-witted verbal abuse because it filled your rotten brain with some sense of superiority. You ridiculed him because you're too stupid to answer his questions. You made him doubt his worth because you thought it might vindicate yours. Have you ever wondered how many students you'd have if they actually wanted to learn? Zero, because you have nothing to teach. Imagine an empty classroom: no one laughing at your idiotic jokes, no one helping you pretend you're not really just a bum, lower than anyone you've ever degraded. The boy you tried to injure yesterday is more of a man than you'll ever be."

Kevin knew the inevitable consequence of the mounting fury in Brandt's eyes, and stood in anticipation of it. The big man's upper lip curled, and with the mindless ferocity of a cornered animal, he charged. Kevin took one step forward and one to the side and drove his right palm into the center of the big man's back, sending him headlong and sprawling across the floor.

"I don't give a sweet damn how it happened!" yelled Mr. Saunders. "You shouldn't have provoked him. You know he has a temper."

Kevin stared across the dining room, stoically silent.

"First, you take off without a word to your mother and me. Then you skip school. Then, your first day back, you assault a teacher in front of his class. I've had it! This time I've *really* had it! As of right now you're going to straighten up. You're going to stop arguing with your teachers, you're going to stop screwing around with your tests, and you're going to start treating Capital City High with respect.

"To begin with, you're to apologize to Coach Brandt, because as far as I'm concerned, you were riling him deliberately. Second, I expect at least a *C* on your Economics and Environmental Studies midterms next week. Third, you're going to participate in some kind of extracurricular activity. I don't care what it is: Yearbook Staff, Chess Club, Prom Committee, Debate Team, whatever. You're going to start showing some interest in your school. Fourth, I've arranged an appointment with Dr. Minkler first period tomorrow morning. I suggest you go. And finally, from now until you graduate, school comes first, and you'd better not forget it, because if you do, you're out, and if you think it's rough getting a decent job without a college degree, try getting one without a high school diploma."

Kevin skipped dinner and spent the evening in his room. He was still awake reading when the telephone rang at ten-forty-five. It was Dana.

"I heard what happened in school today," Dana said. "Are you alright?"

"I'm fine."

"I don't know what Mr. Sullivan told you, but I worked everything out on my own, and I think I've made the right decision. Do you have a minute?"

"Sure," Kevin answered, marking his place in the book he had been reading and setting it aside.

"Well, Coach Brandt asked what we thought about Selective Service. You know, the draft. I'd been thinking about it a lot lately—I turned eighteen today—but I wasn't sure how to defend my opinion. Now I'm sure. I spent this morning writing everything I could think of about how it's done, why, who's eligible, what's at stake, what it implies. Do you know what I learned?"

"What?"

"It's wrong. I mean *really* wrong. So wrong it's hard to believe possible.

"The most important thing a person has is his life, right? It has to be. I mean, you can love your family or your job or your house, but first you have to be alive. So, life—*your own* life—is the first and most important thing, which means *life* has to be the basis for judging thoughts and actions. I'm sure of this, I've considered it from every angle, and now it's so obvious it's almost embarrassing.

"*I own my life*. It doesn't belong to my family or my neighbors or the government. It's *mine*. I had no idea how much that mattered, Kevin, or even what it felt like to say it. *No one* can own the life of another person, which means no one can claim the right to any life but his own. Forcing a person to risk or lose his life for a cause he may or may not believe in is . . . I don't know what to call it but *evil*.

"If a person values his life he'll fight to keep it, by choice. If he believes that some threat is worth the cost of war, he'll go to war. But if he doesn't think it's worth going to war, what value is he to the fight if he has to be forced to serve it? And it doesn't matter what the cause is, either, or whose it is, or even *why* it is. Those things may be important, but they're not the basis for questions about whether Selective Service, or any compulsory service, is right or wrong. What matters is that a person's first responsibility is to what makes everything in his world possible: his life. The rest has to be judged by that. Whether to fight for his life, or run for his life. And those judgments can be made *only* by the owner of the life.

"The real question is: Can anyone own the life of another person? Yes? Or no? Not occasionally or sometimes or during a government-declared emergency, but one or the other. Yes? Or no?

"Selective Service means *yes*."

Kevin was smiling. "That's great, Dana," he said. "You should be proud of yourself."

"And, you know, I'm not going to register, either, even if they put me in jail."

Kevin considered for a moment, then asked, "Are you sure?"

"Well, Selective Service is wrong. Wouldn't registering be the same as approving?"

"I don't think so. I don't think that obeying an order under the threat of personal harm is an approval. I agree that you—we—should do what we can to fight something so wrong, but if you believe what you said about the importance of life, and you're forced to choose between two wrongs, I think you should make your decision according to the likelihood of a threat to your life."

There was a moment's silence before Dana replied. "You're right," he said, his tone slightly despondent. "How did you know that so easily?"

Kevin laughed. "I have an older brother. I thought about it when *he* registered without thinking about it," he answered. "Will you be in school tomorrow?"

"Yes. I missed a Trig quiz today. I hope he'll let me make it up. It's Mr. VanAnglin, you know."

"Probably he will. But isn't what you learned worth a quiz or two?"

"Yes."

"I'll see you in Environmental Studies. Happy birthday, Dana."

Dr. Minkler was at her desk when Kevin entered. He seated himself in a chair across from her, opened his notebook, and resumed work on an unfinished calculus problem. Several minutes passed, and it was Dr. Minkler who broke the silence.

"So . . ." she said, rubbing her palms together, "what would you like to talk about?"

Kevin paused long enough to complete a notation, then looked up and replied, "Nothing."

"What about your future?"

"What about it?"

"I understand you're going to have one of the highest midyear grades Mr. VanAnglin has ever given. Do you have any interest in becoming a mathematician?"

"No."

"How about a mechanic?"

He inclined his head but said nothing. She avoided his gaze.

"Have you considered being a football coach? You were quite the star last year. Or maybe you'd like to get into the retail business. Maybe manage a bookstore?"

She shrugged in the continuing silence and studied her desk. She leafed absentmindedly through the material neatly arranged across it.

"Oh," she said, "I almost forgot. Have you seen these?"

She opened a drawer and removed three envelopes.

"Your father sent the applications in about six weeks ago," she said extending her hand. "Hanover turned you down and so did Middlebury, but not Shenandoah."

He accepted the envelopes and glanced at each of them briefly. "Why Shenandoah?" he asked.

"Their requirements are a little less rigid, and they have a harder time meeting their out-of-state quota."

"No, I mean why Shenandoah as a school?"

"Ah," she said, "that was *my* suggestion."

Kevin decided not to ask the question again. He folded the Shenandoah envelope into his shirt pocket and dropped the other two on Dr. Minkler's desk. She reached into another drawer and withdrew a glossy white folder with a large green S ornately embossed over a blue mountain range.

"For you," she explained, handing him the folder.

"Thanks," he said.

"Is there anything else you'd like to talk about?"

"Such as?"

"I don't know. Problems. Challenges. In school. At home. Anything you like."

"No," he answered, rising and walking to the door. "But you can tell my father I'll be going to college."

Daniel returned alone to Jenness Beach before dawn on Friday morning. The warm front had passed, and he sat parked in Rebecca's car with the front windows down, hoping the cold air might clear his head, wishing she believed in him.

They had engaged in several long conversations since Kevin's departure, but always there seemed a trace of doubt in her eyes, like a question unasked, or a lingering suspicion. He wondered, after the pain his distance had caused her, what he could say to prove what he'd learned. Now that he was certain his plans were possible, what could he do to regain her trust?

He could, he suddenly realized, let her read his journal. He could let her see what he had been thinking, discover what he had discovered. She would know what he knew, and in knowing she would realize how difficult the learning had been. She would know his mind by journeying into it.

He smiled. Finally, he thought, she would know his admiration of her paintings. And she would read—

His enthusiasm crumpled. She would read what he had come to think of as *the gray pages*. The writing he had refused to believe because it seemed too horrible to be true. The writing he could not doubt because the evidence was all around him.

No, he decided, he would not let her read his journal, and he would not rend pages from it. He would prove his sincerity by his actions, the proof that ultimately mattered most. At least, he acknowledged in consolation, Kevin believed in him.

"Fellow educators, members of the press, boys and girls of Capital City High School: please welcome United States Secretary of Education Albert Winfield."

With the exception of Dr. Minkler, not a single person in the gymnasium understood what was happening. The Department of Education's sporadically placed, specifically tenuous press releases had divulged little more than the title of a reformative new system and, conditioned by the emptiness of past reform rumors, not even those who listened took the news seriously. The consensus was an impression that the school was being honored, and that it must be an illustrious honor since the country's head of education had come to bestow it. An indecisive applause emboldened itself into a hearty welcome as a professorial mid-sixties man sporting silver-rimmed spectacles and a silver-streaked goatee stepped to the lectern.

"Thank you, Dr. Minkler," the man said in a velvety tone. "Thank you, everyone. It is indeed a pleasure to be here today because I come as the bearer of good news. In fact, for those of us in education, long-overdue good news. I'm here to introduce to you the New American People's Educational System. You're here as one of twelve specially chosen schools that will introduce the system to America and the world. Its success depends on you, and I might add that I, personally, after having had several wonderful conversations with your own Dr. Minkler, am brimming with hope for the future of Capital City High. Believe me, by your participation in this revolutionary new concept, you will soon be a part of this great country's heritage, and you will proudly blaze the trail along which an entire nation shall follow."

He paused expectantly and nodded gratefully during a short applause, then proceeded.

"One of the most important things for you to keep in mind is that truly significant change seldom happens overnight. It takes time and patience and dedicated effort. Is that not correct? Well, many of you will have graduated before the results of your dedication bear fruit, so we must continually keep in mind that this system can never be expected to succeed if all we're thinking about is what *we* get out of it. The future of our country is at stake, because sooner than you realize it will be in *your* hands, and that's a solemn responsibility. *Now* is the time to prepare. *Now* is the time to set the stage for the future.

"Education..." he said reverently, floating the word over his audience. "Education is vital, so vital that without it almost nothing is possible. That little fact is the founding principle on which we are building the New American People's Educational System—and that's a solid foundation. Until now, the problems we have faced in education seemed, oddly enough, to multiply in the face of our previous moderate solutions. America's illiteracy rate has tripled over the last twenty years, social attitudes are at an all-time low, and students are emerging from school less and less educated. This is a trend that has to be stopped, and the New American People's Educational System is the cure. Allow me to tell you about it.

"First, as with anything, where there's good news there's not-so-good news. There are two sides to every coin. Are there not? The not-so-good news is that you are all going to have to work just a little bit harder. The good news is that your hard work is going to pay off in ways you've probably never imagined. For example, starting next quarter, junior and senior students will have free access to community job-placement services through your school's guidance department. Local businesses hiring high-school students will be awarded special tax consideration, and younger students will have a chance to partake of various community services for credit. Additionally, we anticipate being able to offer better-than-ever government loans for college, as well as vocational training and a federally funded scholarship incentive for the two best students, one boy and one girl."

He paused to review the notes he had spread across the lectern.

"Okay . . ." he said after finding what he needed. "Obviously we're not going to go and change your curriculum right in the middle of the school year, but I'd like to take a minute to encapsulate next year's changes. Again, there's good news and not-so-good news. I'll commence with the latter. More English, but with emphasis on two completely new areas: journalism studies and cultural-flexibility workshops, because we all know the importance of proper news interpretation, and we all need to keep abreast of our ever-changing world. More political science so that you can fully understand the workings of your government. More economics so that you can fully understand the world of business and finance. And more psychology so that we can fully understand each other.

"Now for the good news. There will be less ancient,

unrelated history. Instead you'll be studying current events —recent history, if you will—and the activities that affect you directly. How's that sound?"

There was an agreeable applause; several students whistled. Winfield smiled and waited.

"There will be less abstract scientific theory and more environmental studies. Less structure, more see-and-do, because there's nothing like hands-on learning, and there's more than enough to discover right here in your own back yard. You'll have more vocational classes to choose from, because there are many students who don't want to go to college, and that's okay, because our country needs skilled laborers as much as it needs white-collar workers. You'll see improved sports programs and a wider variety of activities in physical education: weight lifting, aerobics, bicycling, dancing—even swimming, because everyone should know how to swim. Now, I'm not saying you'll get your own pool ..." He tittered with the audience before adding, "Wouldn't that be something! But you will be able to enjoy regularly scheduled trips to a community pool.

"Finally, there'll be three major format changes. The first will be a wider application of what we like to call group-perspective grading. Some of you may know it as grading on a curve. After all, we're in school to learn, not to be judged in competition against our peers. The second will be the fostering of partnership study and group projects, because we all know that no man is an island, and that America was built by teamwork. We must learn to work together while we're young, before it becomes too late for us to change. We must learn to help others and to accept help without letting pride get in our way, and if your generation can master that now, imagine how much easier it will be for generations to come! And third, poor grades will no longer be considered sufficient cause for holding students back, because research has shown that children who are prevented from advancing with their peers suffer irreparable psychological damage and a drastically diminished sense of confidence, often eliminating their chances for positive future development while destroying their self-esteem.

"Now, there's one thing I'd like to explain to teachers and those representatives of the press who have joined us here today. You are no doubt wondering why I would unveil the details of this plan to a gymnasium full of students before disclosing them to you. The answer, really, is quite simple.

"Our educational system needs help. The young people here today are the innocent victims of what I like to call, 'program insufficiency.' On that basis, I believe *they* should be the first to know. We can't go on treating our students like second-rate citizens. They, too, have rights, and it's *their* interest which we must serve. Is it not?

"And so I say to the young men and women of Capital City High School: You are among the chosen. The future is in your hands. Good luck!"

Winfield stepped back from the lectern and bowed to a fervent applause. Mr. Saunders joined him a moment later and shook his hand, exaggerating his grin and prolonging their grip for a photographer.

"Thank you, Mr. Winfield," he exclaimed. "Okay everybody, calm down and listen up. Third period doesn't start for almost ten minutes, and at that time Mr. Winfield will be answering questions for the press and teachers. Until then, he has offered to take questions from the student body. Please keep them brief and to the point. Those of you having class next period with . . ." He glanced at a limp square of paper in his palm. "Mrs. Turcotte, Miss Lambert, Mr. VanAnglin, Mrs. LeFabvre, Mr. Whithers, and Mrs.

Clement, please report to the cafeteria for a study hall. Okay, go ahead with your questions."

"Yes," Winfield said into the microphone while pointing toward the uppermost row of bleachers. "The young man in the dark sweater."

Kevin lowered his hand and stood, backlighted by a wide spread of east-facing windows. He spoke slowly and clearly, and with just enough volume to be heard throughout the gymnasium.

"You will never get away with this."

Asked Samuel Finch, a reporter for the *Concord Mirror*: "There are thousands of other schools you could have chosen as one of the twelve. What is it about Capital City High that makes it special?"

Winfield smiled empathetically and answered, "Absolutely everything."

Asked Mrs. LeFabvre, head of Capital City's English Department: "Are you saying that the entire educational system will eventually come under federal supervision?"

Winfield shrugged dismissively and answered, "In a sense, yes, but each community will continue to maintain its own board of educational representatives."

Asked Mr. Whithers, head of Capital City's Vocational Programs Department: "Does that mean we'll be getting more federal money?"

Winfield nodded enthusiastically and answered, "I meant what I said about education receiving *top* priority. You'll get as much federal money as you need."

Asked Mrs. Clement, head of Capital City's Science

Department: "Will that mean better salaries for teachers?"

Winfield answered genially, "Of course. Teachers will be paid on a scale equivalent to many of the high-tech positions competing with their profession."

Asked Martin Bannion, Director of the Merrimack Public Schools Administration Unit: "What about private schools?"

Winfield answered patronizingly, "We all know how private schools create an unfair advantage for the children of wealthy parents, but we must keep in mind that they're merely a phenomenon stemming from the shortcomings in our present system. Given the extraordinarily high standards of our new program, I estimate that within four years there will no longer be any market for private schools. Why would anyone want to pay all that money when the finest education is available for free?"

Asked Lana Fitzwater, a newswoman for Nashua Civic Television: "I'm impressed by the efficacy with which the government has acted in coming to the aid of our failing educational system. Usually even the simplest programs take forever to be actualized. Why the exception in this case?"

Winfield answered without expression, "We understand the nature of the problem, and it would be a dereliction of duty to let it get out of hand. As hard as we have tried in the past, it should be obvious by now that anything less than total support is insufficient support. Partial measures yield partial results, I always say. Public education is more than just a tradition in America, it's a way of life, a provider of futures, a symbol of equality, a right. You may rest assured, ladies and gentlemen, that should anything threaten this new program—which, I can state unequivocally, is at the heart of America's future—our government can and will act with incredible swiftness."

Daniel was standing on the sidewalk outside the bookstore when Kevin closed for the night.

"Hello!" Kevin exclaimed, happily surprised.

"Hello," said Daniel warmly. "How have you been?"

"Great. I've been considering what you said about grading writing in every class. Do you mean giving two separate grades? One for the subject and one for the writing?"

"No. One grade."

"What about students who know the material yet have difficulty expressing it in writing? I know students who—"

"I understand. Given the average teacher's imprudent regard for writing, it's a predictable condition. But if writing was taught as an integral part of every subject at the outset, knowledge and the concise expression of it would go hand in hand."

Kevin nodded, then locked the bookstore door and turned and asked, "What brings you to Concord?"

"I told Rebecca I was going for a drive. I thought perhaps I could persuade you to ride back with me."

"Really? I wish I could, but I have to open in the morning. What about Sunday? It's a three-day weekend."

"I ship out Sunday at dawn, though I'm sure it would be fine with Rebecca."

"You're leaving? I thought—"

"I'll be back the first week of April, to stay. We'll have the whole summer."

"Why go at all?"

"I can't just walk out on Captain Reneau, and I could

use a couple of months to finish my plans." He smiled and added, "You were the spark I needed."

"But . . . Rebecca—"

"I know. Take care of yourself, okay?"

"I will," Kevin replied, gripping Daniel's offered hand. "I'll see you in April. Maybe you can come to my graduation!"

Daniel laughed and said, "Maybe."

15

REBECCA NOLAN

Kevin closed his notebook, then his eyes. It was not, he realized, Winfield's speech that disturbed him, but the automatized manner in which the audience had responded to it. It was as if his fellow students had opened their mouths to receive a substance resembling food and then swallowed, not because they knew it was food, but because they were told it was food. And when told that it might not be good for them, but that it would be good for the next round of swallowers, they believed.

Had they lost their sense of taste? he wondered. Or had they never acquired one? Perhaps they didn't care what they were fed so long as they were spared the effort of selection and chewing, so long as all they had to do was swallow.

Was the analogy that simple?

No, he decided. But it *was* as simple as to think or not.

He wished they could know the importance of their minds. He wished they could understand that everything they are and everything they will ever become depends upon their ability to think for themselves and the quality of their thinking, and upon the extent to which they own their thoughts and minds.

Their *lives*, he amended.

Throughout childhood he had heard: "That boy has a mind of his own." Eventually he began to question the alternative. Were there people whose minds were not their own? Did some people's minds belong to someone else?

What if his fellow students had been presented with Daniel's words instead of Winfield's? Or if they could hear the ideas of one and then the ideas of the other? What if they were given the chance to compare and judge? If they fully understood what was at stake, he wondered, what would they choose?

Fragmented thoughts and pictures, like a scattering of puzzle pieces, swarmed his mind in search of connection: Winfield's speech . . . Selective Service . . . Ms. Barrymore's protest . . . Phillip Sparrow's concert . . . Mr. Sullivan's test idea . . .

"Good morning."

He looked up to see Rebecca standing in the aisle at the front of the motionless bus, smiling. She wore a trim down parka in ivory with a pale-green scarf and matching beret. Her cheeks were scarlet from the cold.

"This *is* your stop isn't it?" she asked playfully, glancing left and right at the empty seats.

From the downtown station they strolled along Marcy Street and Strawberry Banke to Prescott Park, where she ran ahead down the winding snow-packed walkway to the foot of a giant elm. Two colossal limbs spread perpendicular to the trunk, just beyond reach of her raised hands.

"What are you doing?" Kevin asked when he caught up with her.

She unwrapped the scarf from around her neck, rolled it into a ball, and tossed it high into the tree. It struck a branch and partially unfurled, then snagged ten feet above them.

"Nice throw!" he commended flippantly. "Now what?"

She grinned. "The Tree Climbing Championships of the World. First one to the scarf, wins."

He laughed. "Are you serious?"

"If I win, you have to make lunch. If you win, I have to hang your graduation tassel from the mirror in my car."

He paused in mock contemplation. "Okay," he agreed, "you're on. Which branch do you want?"

"It doesn't matter."

"Do you want a head start?"

"It won't be necessary."

"How 'bout a boost?"

"I don't think I can lift you," she retorted, rolling her eyes. "Ready? One . . . Two . . . Three!"

Kevin jumped and clutched the higher of the limbs, hooking one leg over the top and hoisting himself into a sitting position. When he reached for the branch closest to the scarf he saw Rebecca standing in the snow two paces back from the trunk of the tree, smirking deviously, shaping with her hands a snowball the size of an orange.

"You wouldn't . . ." he protested.

She nodded, and with a confident sweep of her arm she hurled the projectile. He ducked reflexively as the sphere sailed passed and hit the scarf, and he watched as it floated into Rebecca's waiting hands. She draped it around her neck and ran away laughing down the path. A minute later he found her bundled against the wind on a bench facing the harbor.

"I had no intention of hanging one of those things from my mirror," she bantered, still smiling. "I hope you can cook."

"And I hope *you* like peanut-butter sandwiches," he

parried, sitting beside her. "Tell me, what's your middle name?"

"Wysteria," she replied, facing him. "Why do you ask?"

His smile was a laugh turned inward, silent and musingly secretive.

"Why are you smiling?" she asked.

"The turquoise waves . . . the transitioning sky . . . the hourglass brimming with gold."

Her eyes narrowed, then opened wide. "You've seen it?" she inquired excitedly.

"I own it."

She stared at him for a long time, then rose as if entranced and crossed to the balustrade at the water's edge. Her fingers and cheeks were numb from the wind. She began to shiver.

"How long have you known it was mine?" she asked, staring into the distance over the harbor.

"Six days."

"How long have you owned it?"

"Since November."

He came to her as she turned, her gaze seeking and embracing his. When they kissed it seemed almost as if their mouths never met, as if the source of their pleasure was only the unwavering sight of each in the other's eyes. After a while she said quietly, her lips barely separated from his, "I painted that after I moved here with Daniel. It was the first one I sold."

She drew a tremulous composing breath. She tilted her head back and looked up at him. "Do you know what pleases me most?" she asked. "That meeting the artist has not been a disappointment for you, and that you've seen me, in a very real sense, naked. I . . . I haven't stopped thinking about the way you looked at my painting in the gallery last week."

Propped on one elbow, she studied him lying on his back beside her, clothed only in the shadows of dusk. A gray flannel sheet and white down comforter trailed on the floor at the foot of her bed.

"Aren't you cold?" he asked.

"No," she replied, rolling over him, pinning him beneath her torso and legs. "Are you?"

"Not any more," he whispered against her neck.

"What have you been thinking?"

"I was trying to picture you as a student in high school. Did you have many friends?"

"No. There were students I liked but there was never any real closeness."

"Did that bother you?"

"Sometimes. Why do you ask?"

"Often I wonder why it doesn't bother me. So many people worry about being liked."

"And about 'fitting in'?"

"Especially that."

"Actually," she said after a thoughtful interval, "there *was* something that bothered me."

"What?" He clasped his hands behind her lower back.

"I couldn't have identified it then, but I never admired anyone my age." She frowned in recollection. "The most popular boy at my high school in Erie was Gordon Merrill. He played football, basketball, baseball, and guitar. He was handsome and well-mannered; his teachers liked him. Everyone liked him. We went out once to dinner and a movie, and all I can remember of our date was that he seemed not to have a single opinion of his own about any-thing. He agreed with whatever I said. It was enlightening to discover that the most popular boy in school didn't stand out from the crowd. He *was* the crowd."

"He sounds like who my father would like me to be."

"What about your mother?"

"She thinks I'm too serious."

"I heard that, too, though not from my mother. The louder you laugh, the more fun you're having. Isn't that what they think?"

"Do they think?"

"They say: 'Why don't you loosen up and have a good time?'"

He laughed. "That's what they say."

"How do you reply?"

"To that?"

"Yes."

"I don't."

"You should."

"Why? If people believe happiness can be had by imi-tating its symptoms, it's not my concern."

"But if you don't challenge that kind of—" She paused thoughtfully. "Kevin, why do you go to the trouble of questioning your teachers? Why do you ask for explana-tions or object when you think something is wrong? Is it because you want to argue?"

"No."

"Is it because you seek the admiration of your class-mates?"

He made a face as if at an absurdity.

"Then, why?" she repeated.

Because, he thought, so much of what is taught *should* be questioned. So much of it seems pointless, even wrong. But that wasn't quite what he wanted to say.

"Wouldn't it be easier to keep silent?" she asked.

"Probably."

"If some politician introduced a law that would harm a business you owned, would you oppose him?"

"Of course."

"Why?"

"To protect my business."

"To protect it from what?"

"From the idea that—"

"From *what*?"

He nodded slowly, then smiled and said with emphasis, "From the *idea*."

"Wrong ideas can only be fought with right ideas. If you're certain that a wrong idea is being expressed—whether wrong means bad, dangerous, evil, or unjust—it's in *your* interest to challenge it. If you're uncertain about the validity of an idea—whether it's being taught in class or imposed on your life—it's in your interest to question it. And if the answer doesn't make sense, it's in your interest to challenge it until it does, or to reject it as invalid. Maybe your challenge won't stop a wrong idea from becoming a wrong action, but maybe it will."

"Thanks for answering what you asked me."

"You knew the answer, you just didn't have the words. Teachers are obligated to know what they teach and why they teach it. Students are responsible for holding teachers to that obligation. Not because students know the answers—they don't—but because their *job* is to understand the answers.

"If the purpose of education is anything less than to teach children how to think for themselves—which means employing teachers who not only know what they teach and why, but who encourage questions and challenges—the result of education will be a society of adults waiting to be told what to do. Despite propaganda to the contrary, an obedient society is the goal of public education, whether or not the better teachers recognize it." She paused. "I had a history teacher at Capital—I can't remember his name. Mr. Parker? . . . Parson? . . ."

"Persons."

"Right. The first day of class he asked us to describe what we liked and didn't like about New Hampshire. The majority favored the mountains and the seashore; cold winters and 'not enough to do' were the most common grievances. I said I liked New Hampshire's motto, *Live Free or Die*, and that I thought state-owned liquor stores were a bad idea, especially at highway rest areas. Mr. What's-His-Name assured me that the motto wasn't meant to be taken literally, that things have changed since Patrick Henry and John Stark, and that liquor sales were important to revenue. To this day I wish I'd been able to respond to him, to challenge him. I wish I'd known then how to put into words what I wanted to say."

She placed her hands on either side of his shoulders and arched against him, looking into his eyes. She asked with an expectant smile, "What did *you* say when the secretary of education spoke at your school?"

"I told him he'd never get away with it."

"Is that what you believe?"

"Certainly."

"Who will stop him?"

"Daniel, you and I . . . And others."

"What others? Who can you name?"

She crawled backwards above him, kissing his chest, his abdomen, his right thigh and knee, then she reached over the footboard for the sheet and adjusted it to cover them both.

"My Auto Shop teacher," he answered, "my Calculus

teacher. There are others. As soon as people realize that this new system is nothing more than a way for the government to gain control over their lives—"

"It's not a new system, Kevin. It's what we have now, what we've had for decades, made explicit. Who challenges the government's authority to enforce compulsory education? Who challenges its authority to tax citizens to pay for public schools whether or not they have children attending those schools?"

He didn't answer.

"More and more," she said, "anyone who challenges that authority is labeled an extremist or a radical or anti-government." She smiled. "I like Daniel's definition of extremist."

"What is it?"

"'Anyone who says *yes* or *no* and means it.' Daniel helped me understand the insidiousness of public education by comparing it to Social Security. Americans accepted a mandatory government program that confiscates their earnings and holds those earnings inaccessible until trickled out at the confiscator's discretion. Daniel asked, 'How could people place so little value on their work and time as to allow their *servants* to seize their savings? Who could care so little about what's best for his life as to allow others to decide it for him?'

"And today, people don't question or challenge Social Security. They accept it automatically. And unless they're self-employed they never even see what's stolen and 'set aside' for their and everyone else's future. It's harder not to question it when you're forced to write a check every year."

"Is that what you do?"

"It's what I'm supposed to do. The point is, a nation of free individuals accepted Social Security, government-controlled education, welfare schemes, and a host of laws and regulations that steal their freedom and perpetuate the idea that the government is, and should be, their parent. What's going to enliven them to reject this alleged new system?"

"Whatever's left of their regard for their freedom."

"And who will teach them how to use what's left?"

"I already told you," he answered, sliding from underneath her and sitting at the edge of the bed. He bent to gather his clothes from the floor and stood to dress.

"Where are you going?" she asked.

"I have to study."

"Would you like me to make dinner?"

"No, thank you. Maybe later."

"Kevin," she said, reaching for his hand, "don't be angry. I only want you to realize that it's not a fight easily won."

"I'm not angry," he assured her. "And I think I know how hard it's going to be."

"And do you also know that we're on the same side?"

He squeezed her hand and knelt beside her. "Of course I know," he replied. He leaned, kissed her mouth, and confirmed, "I've seen your paintings."

16

MODUS VIVENDI

Mr. Saunders paced nervously in the teacher's lounge. "Where the hell is VanAnglin?" he erupted. "Doesn't anybody have a copy of his midterms?"

"The last time I saw him was Friday morning," said Mrs. LeFabvre, "at the meeting after the assembly. As I recall, he got up and left before it was over."

"Did he speak to any of you over the weekend?"

"He doesn't speak to us during the week," answered Mrs. Clement insipidly.

"What about his desk, his file cabinet? Doesn't anybody have a key?"

"They were unlocked this morning when I checked on his homeroom," said Miss Walters.

"And?"

"Empty. Nothing but school texts and a few stacks of blank paper."

"Jesus! Doesn't anybody have a copy of last year's—or something? Miss Burnette, are you sure he's not home?"

"I've been trying all morning. There's just no answer."

"Try again," he snapped. He whirled on Miss Walters.

"Estelle," he proclaimed, "if we can't get a hold of him by third period we're going to have to use one of your tests or a text review. Run something off, will you? And let's keep this thing quiet. Goddamn him!"

To the bewilderment of Mrs. Turcotte and the vexation of Ms. Barrymore, Kevin achieved perfect scores in under twenty minutes on his Economics and Environmental Studies midterms. As expected, he did equally well in Auto Shop and College English, but he took a zero on the last-minute Calculus exam assembled by Miss Walters, leaving on his desk a blank worksheet under the pencil she had issued, broken in half.

Mr. VanAnglin never returned.

Throughout February, Dr. Minkler occupied her time with a single boastfully confidential project. To the occasional inquiry regarding her work she would say, "A smooth transition makes a superior system superior," and although no one knew what she meant it seemed obvious that *she* knew, and no further questions were asked. In early March she announced the creation of CONFER—the Cooperative Network for Educational Restoration—an organization comprised of teachers, parents, and community leaders, with a representative delegation of college-bound students. The governor's name appeared beneath a likeness of the American flag on the group's letterhead. Secretary Winfield recommended forming similar organizations at the other Phase One schools, and Dr. Minkler sent their community-relations directors complimentary copies of her CONFER guidebook.

Complying with his father's order to participate in an extracurricular activity, Kevin joined the Capital City High Chess Club. Once a week he played Dana Brissette, enjoying both the game and their conversation. Mr. Saunders was overjoyed with Kevin's tractable behavior, but when Mrs. Turcotte one day offhandedly remarked, "I'll be glad when that boy graduates," he wasn't sure what to think. He declined to countermand Kevin's refusal to apologize to Coach Brandt.

On the last day of March, Mr. Sullivan announced his resignation.

"Why now?" Kevin asked when he heard. "I mean, couldn't you wait until the end of the year?"

"No," Mr. Sullivan answered, taking a pencil from the top drawer of his desk and rolling it back and forth between his thumb and forefinger. His tone was strained; his face showed fatigue. "Don Whithers vetoed my test idea, and Superintendent Butterworth said it would be inconsistent with that New American People's thing. He said it would 'provoke' competition. He said students need to be treated with 'greater-than-ever equality,' and that it would be unfair to offer 'select' students a chance at higher grades when the rest have 'enough trouble already.'

"Can you imagine? *Unfair* to offer opportunity because some students don't have the capacity or desire to achieve it? Do you have any idea what kind of world this would be without opportunities to rise above the average? The common? The good enough? Can you imagine total stagnation?

"Kevin, how fair would it be for average men to prescribe limitations on the work of exceptional men? Should a talented motor designer be held to the standards of a career tire changer?

"I wanted to encourage inspired students to set above-average goals, not to oppress average students. I wanted to help them discover the rewards of independent effort and accomplishment. Unfair? Bullshit! Where there is more to be gained there is potentially more to be lost. Risk comes with every endeavor—greater goals are balanced by the possibility of greater losses. Students taking advanced-level tests would have had a chance at a better score, but would also have lost more points per error than if they'd taken the basic test. It all worked out. The ratio was there. I honestly thought . . ."

He frowned at the bits of yellow paint beneath his thumbnail. He opened the drawer and returned the pencil.

"Kevin, something is wrong, something I never saw before. Why tinker with tests when tests aren't the problem? Why build cars for performance when the roads are posted, 'five miles an hour, passing prohibited'?" He shook his head. "I'll find a good job with a good business and better pay, and I'll know I've made the right decision. Of course, I'll miss the things that have made this profession worthwhile."

He smiled and said with particular earnestness, "I'll miss *you.*"

Third quarter ended. Aside from occasional modest press attention, the New American People's Educational System caused few discernible changes in the day-to-day operation of Capital City High School. Replacements were found for Mr. Sullivan and Mr. VanAnglin—teachers with spotless reputations, recommended by Secretary Winfield himself, and Dr. Minkler authored a report entitled, "Signs of Success."

For the first time since the concert in Boston, Kevin listened to the music of Phillip Sparrow. Lying on his back on the floor of his room, he felt contentment in the knowledge that the months had finally passed, that tomorrow Daniel would be home. As the second movement of "Sparrow's Flight" began, as the pulse of breaking waves rose and fell within the music, he turned his head to face Rebecca's painting.

It was strange, he thought, that everything he detested ceased to matter. Tonight, it seemed, he could forgive it all. His father, Mrs. Turcotte, Dr. Minkler, Phillip Sparrow —they just hadn't known what was possible, they had never been taught, and perhaps they weren't to blame. Soon, he knew, it would be different. The next generation, at least, would have a chance to learn.

17

THE GRAY PAGES

*T*hrough an open window on the bridge of the *Saint Sal Malone*, blinking into a tepid April rain, Captain Brevard Reneau stared blankly toward Portsmouth Harbor. Beyond the crest of the ship's vacant bow the New England coast spread before him as a pallid smudge. Whaleback Light throbbed feebly over nebulous dock lamps at New Castle and Gerrish Island. Darkness settled beneath gathering clouds as the light of day yielded once more to the lights of men.

It was still drizzling when Kevin and Rebecca met Reneau on the *Sal Malone* Sunday morning.

"I should have telephoned sooner," the captain said apologetically, standing beside a compact steel desk in the office half of his cabin, "but I didn't know what to tell you. It would have been easier if something had happened to him—an accident or something. . . . Anything."

His voice faded and Rebecca glanced at Kevin leaning against the open door, his arms folded and his head down.

"Did you ever read that journal of his?" Reneau asked.

She shook her head.

"Did he ever mention the time he attacked one of my crew for opening the chest where he kept it?"

"No."

"I've seen a lot of scrapes in my time, but this . . . this was merciless, vindictive. It took four men to pull him off the poor bastard. After that, everyone wanted to know what was in his book, and by then I couldn't help wondering if it might be some sort of information for another company, or—"

He broke off, shrugging. His smile was one of dismay.

"I don't know, Miss Nolan. For the life of me I couldn't figure what anyone would want from the *Sal Malone* other than her cargo, and that's never been anything secret or of unusual value, but I was actually starting to wonder if Daniel might know something about the ship that I didn't. I realize how foolish that must sound, but he was an unusual man. *Is* an unusual man. And I knew nothing about him at the time. I guess I convinced myself it was my right, even my responsibility, to find out what was in that book. So, one day . . . I deceived him.

"We were docked at San Sebastian and all the crew had gone ashore except your brother. I asked if he'd run a few errands for me in the city. He obliged; I sent for a locksmith. After mess that night he came to my cabin and asked if I knew who had been reading his journal. I felt like a thief, like I deserved what he gave that sailor, yet I looked him in the eye and said *no*."

Rebecca smiled faintly and shook her head. "If Daniel had wanted anyone to see his journal, it would have been you. I really don't think—"

"Thank you Miss Nolan, but that's not the point, and I believe you know it. All my life I've told the truth, and I'll never forgive myself for lying to your brother, but do you know what was harder to bear than that guilt? What I couldn't ask about what I'd read. I'd never seen anything like it! That book was full of answers, some a few words long, some ten or twelve pages, but there weren't any questions. It was as though he'd asked in his head and answered on the paper. And I'd never before read such writing—as clear as coordinates on a chart. Every word of it made sense and every—"

"Please, sir," Rebecca interrupted, "where is he?"

Reneau nodded, and from a drawer in his desk he removed a large manila envelope and a folded sheet of lined yellow paper. He handed both to Rebecca.

She unfolded and flattened the paper over the envelope and turned to face Kevin, still leaning against the door.

"Captain Reneau," she read quietly, "when my sister finds I have not returned she will come to you. I once promised her an explanation for my inconsistency—a promise, it seems, I lack the courage to break. I regret leaving her with the contents of this envelope, which I trust you will deliver. Thank you for giving me the sea."

She looked from the paper to Kevin and said, "It's signed *DN*." Again she asked Reneau, "Where is he?"

Two small puddles had formed side by side on the floor beneath the chair over which the captain had draped his slicker. With the toe of his right boot he drew a connecting line from one to the other.

"Between Scylla and Charybdis," he mumbled listlessly.

"What?" Kevin asked.

Reneau sighed and raised his head. "Daniel left the ship in Lisbon, Miss Nolan. Almost a month ago. He could be anywhere by now."

The unsealed envelope contained pages torn from the binding of Daniel's journal. The white cotton stock was water spotted and dog-eared but the handwriting was perfectly legible. Rebecca sat on the living-room floor with her legs outstretched and crossed, reclining against the sofa, resting her head on Kevin's thigh as he read aloud.

"Because achievement, independence, and liberty are not what they desire.

"I hear it in their words. I see it in their eyes. Not despair for having failed after a commitment to honest effort, but something worse: a shameful resentment toward those who have, with honest effort, achieved. They don't want to achieve, they want only to have. They don't aspire to independence and liberty, independence and liberty impose too great a responsibility. They don't even want to pursue happiness, they want happiness handed to them.

"They are the final soulless product of an antimind education, the link between upright reasoning man and housebroken primates. They are, and have been throughout history, mankind's destroyer.

"How can one fight an enemy whose code defines self-immolation? What strategy can one use in a battle against a lifeless opponent?

"I do not know.

"The government of the first nation on Earth created by and for free individuals has disintegrated into a cabal salivating at the thought of ruling an impotent collective. The seeds of their opportunity were planted long ago; at last they've amassed their majority. A manifesto emanates from the public pit:

> "Censor this book so our children can't read it,
> Outlaw that thought so our neighbors can't think it.
> Give us our bread, we have to eat better,
> Then feed the whole world, we're in this together.

> "Ban that idea, we don't want to believe it,
> Tax other men harder, we vote they don't need it.
> In foreign affairs be completely forgiving,
> Turn cheek after cheek, say we're sorry for living.

> "Hold up our failures, our sex, and our race
> As standards of virtue in setting man's pace.
> Oh, please, Mother State, use your almighty lever,
> Give us what we desire and we'll serve you forever.

"For every one man who has earned, a hundred wish only to have. For every one man who knows pride, a hundred know envy much better. For every one man who loves life, a hundred merely fear death. For every one man who asks *why*, ten thousand do not and obey.

"See how they flee from the truth! They get drunk, stoned, high, wasted, fucked-up, shit-faced, plastered, mellow, bombed, and buzzed—for what? Is consciousness so difficult a state for them to bear? Is reality so unendurable? What a pathetic condition they enjoy. What an eloquent self-image they confess.

"I waited in a checkout line at a grocery store behind a mother and father and four dirty children. Two of the urchins crawled about the floor, snorting like piglets. An older boy whined in a bored monotone, over and over demanding candy. Their mother's designer sweatshirt bulged in rolls over stretched-out bluejeans; her multicolored manicured fingernails dropped orange crunchies into the mouth of a toddler in a shopping cart. Her husband carefully separated magazines, dog food, cigarettes, and beer from the groceries and paid for them in cash, then carelessly tossed a balled-up booklet of food stamps on the counter for the rest. I seized the wad and tore it to shreds and wished the parasite had attacked me, knowing all the while that this pitiable sight represented a goal, a plan, and if not reversed in time, a future.

"What would an able man do at the outset of his career if he realized that a decade or more of it would be spent cultivating human sponges and perpetuating bottomless failure? Would he cooperate if told he could bring home what he produced Monday through Thursday, but that Fridays did not belong to him? Would he blunder ahead or would he refuse? Would he understand, at that beginning, what his earnings represent? Would he learn?

"There is little time left for him to learn and no one left to teach him.

"The inhabitants of this country sense that something is awry, but they know not what it is and their fumbling remedies are wrong. They are incapable, it would appear, of grasping even the most evident principles, owing, I'm certain, to their blissfully anticonceptual education. Over and over they seek solutions to their problems by addressing the symptoms, or worse.

"Behold, fluttering like a banner over the next Dark Ages, the wonderdrug prescribed by the Surgeons General of the Soul: unconditional love.

"Love is man's greatest emotional response to profoundly important personal values, and, like an honest coin, it must be earned. Unconditional love, *unearned* love —were it not an utter self-negation—makes a travesty of man's capacity to recognize, judge, and honor values. This, as a cure for his troubles, can only annihilate man's spirit and prepare his body for servitude.

"I have known moments when it appeared that my hope for mankind was justified, when it seemed he might finally hold as sovereign the discernment of his rational mind, that reason and persuasion would at last prevail over faith and force, but my hope falters in the shadow of his self-made destroyer. It conjures itself before me as an indefatigable apparition of mutant ideas, a cancerous growth invited, welcomed, and sustained by its victims. Even now, as its corpse-like fingers clutch at the throat of their independence and liberty, men nourish and protect it. How simple it should be to let it die; how devotedly its victims, its hosts, strive to ensure its survival.

"Between the covers of this journal exists a record of the discoveries of my mind. Why, when so much of it has been proof of my strength and source of my happiness, am I incessantly drawn toward the particular despair, the irresolute grayness, of these pages? How is it that I, who have felt for life and learning an indescribable passion, have become consumed by an unendurable abhorrence of most of my own species?

"Why did the finest teacher I ever knew relinquish her career in hopeless frustration? Why did the man who gave me life, who taught me by example its meaning and value, end his own?

"I fear that the world they deserved can never be."

Kevin closed his eyes. The pages slipped from his grasp and fell to the floor.

"I didn't know about my father," Rebecca whispered.

"... and to the republic for which it stands, one nation, under God, indivisible, with liberty, and justice, for all. And now for the morning announcements."

Two thousand students in sixty-four homerooms simultaneously returned to their seats. The female voice resumed its tinny drone.

"Congratulations to Dana Brissette for making valedictorian, and to Mary Jensen, salutatorian. Congratulations to Wanda Bell, Irene Blum, Larry Boatwright, Peter Fortin, Alex Garr, Priscilla Libby, Kevin Saunders, Leslie Topolosky, and Tina Whiting for achieving high honors, and to Eric Dawson and Stevie Cole for their acceptance to DSU. There will be no JV basketball—*baseball*—tonight, but you should bring your cleats tomorrow in case the field is dry. All graduating seniors who have not yet paid for their caps and gowns must do so today, or you will not be allowed to be in the graduation exercises. Also, congratulations to the girls' tennis team for winning their final match. Monday, June— Oh, also, Mr. Saunders would like to remind everyone that even though it's warm outside you still have to eat lunch in the cafeteria. Have a nice day."

Dana Brissette was waiting outside Keven's homeroom when the bell rang.

"Good morning," said Kevin.

"Where are you headed?" asked Dana.

"Calculus."

"I miss VanAnglin."

"So do I."

They walked together down the hall and up the stairs.

Dana stopped at the door to his first class.

"Listen," he said, "I noticed your name wasn't on the cap-and-gown list. I take it you've decided not to participate in the ceremony?"

"That's right," Kevin answered.

"Would you like to be in the audience?"

"Why?"

"Well, from what I understand there's going to be a special attendance this year. Education Secretary Winfield, the mayor, the press, possibly even the governor."

"So?"

"So," Dana riposted with a smile, "I thought you might come for the valediction."

18

VALEDICTION

*I*n a nameless pub on a forgotten lane east of Glasgow, a teenaged girl cleared dishes from a table by a window. She grinned at the sight of an uncommonly generous tip and wished she had given the stranger better service. He hadn't wanted much, she recalled, only to be left alone. As she stooped to lift the dish pail from the floor, she noticed a book on the seat of his pushed-in chair.

"Father," she called across the empty room, "'ave a look. The Yank left 'is diary . . . or somethin'."

"Put it out wi' th' trash," came a gruff reply from the kitchen.

The girl pulled out the chair and retrieved the book and sat with it on her lap. She looked once around the room, turned back the leather cover, and read silently from the top of a random page.

> . . . source, implicit in every lesson, so that
> each might emerge from class, from
> school, from life, the owner of his mind.
> By this, each will learn the value of his

> judgment, the reward of his effort, and the
> inviolable pride in achieving self-set goals.
> By this, each will know life as an end in
> itself, life as the purpose of life, happiness
> as the measure of—

A shadow obscured the handwritten entry and the girl glanced up, hoping for a moment it might be the stranger returned. It was her father.

"You've no business readin' 'at, an' no need! What's 'at money?" he grunted, pointing to the bills on the table.

She smiled, "It's what 'e left for my—"

"Give it 'ere," he spat, snatching it up and holding it to the light. "'Ow come so much?" he prodded distrustfully. "Were you chattin' 'im up? 'Ey?"

"No."

"Where's th' rest of it, then? You 'ad more 'n one table t'night. Ol' man Peachum, Fergie an' 'is wife . . ."

The girl dipped her hand into the pocket of her apron and displayed a palmful of coins. "I thought maybe I could keep some t'night," she said hopefully, "seein' I made so—"

"You thought!" her father guffawed. "Give it 'ere. Now, do like I said wi' 'at book an' finish your work. It's a quarter to midnight an' there's church in th' mornin'."

He turned, counting the change as he left the room, unaware of the peculiar way his daughter stared after him. Furtively, she took a flower from the mason jar in the window and marked the page she had begun reading, then hid the journal beneath a pile of rags at the back of the mop closet.

"Parents and family, Governor Kaufman, Mayor and Mrs. Trumbell, Reverend and Mrs. Holt, faculty, friends, and students: It is with great pleasure that I welcome you to Rumford Field for the ninety-first graduation exercises of Capital City High School. I would like, also, to extend an especially honored welcome to United States Secretary of Education Albert Winfield, who has come all the way from Washington to be here with us today.

"As principal of Capital City High School, I'd like to take a few brief moments to express some of my own, personal sentiments regarding this very special and important occasion. I say *personal* because there have been times when . . ."

Dana Brissette's gaze remained fixed on the person whose attendance he required. Again, he considered his decision; again, he affirmed it. With the resolve of a man who has already jumped, he hoped for the best.

". . . though, naturally, back in those days, kids had fewer choices and less competition, especially when you stop to consider . . ."

Kevin contemplated the folder on his lap, then looked to his left at Rebecca. He had not told her why he wanted her to come, and she had not asked.

". . . I guess it must have been about two years before I was elected mayor, my daughter came up to me and said, 'Dad, I'm really glad you and Mom went to my graduation,' and you know, that made me feel good inside, because deep down . . ."

Mr. Sullivan sat directly in front of the site-assembled stage. He had declined Dana's mailed invitation, but when the boy came to his home to ask again, he accepted.

". . . and I've often been told that I'm wasting my time trying to get these young men and women into college, but I'm very proud to say that, this year, almost fifty-five percent of our graduating seniors have been accepted into schools of higher . . ."

Mr. VanAnglin leaned against the right-field fence, just outside the effective range of the PA system. He, too, had been invited by Dana, but he had no intention of hearing guest speakers.

". . . a man who consistently places the welfare of others before his own personal ambition, a man who has publicly pledged to raise the intellectual level of our country to shimmering new heights: Secretary of Education Albert Winfield."

Time is limited, Kevin thought.

"Thank you, Mr. Butterworth. The New American People's Educational System is not just a dream for the future, it is a dream for today. It is here, it is now, and it has come in the hour of our greatest . . ."

Dana shifted in his seat, listening only for the announcement of his name. He wiped the dampness from his palms and prepared to stand.

". . . for a glorious new future."

After a ratifying applause, Winfield lightened his tone. "And now," he said, "comes the time for what is, perhaps, the most important address given at any school's commencement ceremony—the speech offered to the world by the most successful participant of a system designed to foster success—by a student who has met the challenge of his school and emerged a winner—by a student who knows what it means to earn the respect of his teachers.

"Ladies and gentlemen, it gives me great pleasure to introduce the valedictorian of Capital City High School, Dana Brissette."

Kevin reached for Rebecca's hand. Mr. Sullivan leaned forward in his chair. Mr. VanAnglin approached the crowd.

Dana took the stage and crossed to the lectern. He placed his hands flat upon its polished sloping top, and with only a trace of unsteadiness said into the microphone, "I have wanted to be valedictorian since my freshman year. I have wanted to achieve my school's highest grade-point average. I have wanted to be accepted by my choice of universities. I have wanted the intellectual respect of my teachers and fellow students. I have wanted to stand here on graduation day to deliver the traditional farewell address. I'm happy to say that I have accomplished these goals and that I'm proud of it, but the source of my pride is not what I had expected, and the speech I have in mind will not be traditional."

He paused, shifting his hands to grip the outside edges of the lectern. Kevin rose and began walking toward the stage.

"There is a student here today," Dana recommenced, his voice slightly louder, slightly steadier, "whose presence in class has caused resentment and frustration for all but our best teachers. He is a graduating senior who chose not to participate in this ceremony, until I suggested a reason why he should. When I asked Kevin Saunders if he would write and deliver today's valedictory, he said *yes*. I suggest you listen."

Secretary Winfield cast a befuddled glance at Dr. Minkler, who cast a menacing glance at Mr. Saunders, who cast a troubled glance safely into space.

"Do something, Ed," hissed Dr. Minkler out of the side of her mouth.

"Too late," said Dana as he passed in front of her, nodding to Kevin on the way back to his seat.

"Good afternoon," Kevin began, ignoring the commotion behind him and removing four sheets of paper from the folder he had been carrying. "We have just completed a program of mandatory learning. The cost to us so far has been twelve years of life, twelve years we can never have again. But if what we were taught was wrong or impractical or incomplete or without foundation, the cost will rise and our payments will continue—without our knowledge and to the wrong collectors—until we no longer have the means to pay."

Behind Kevin and slightly to his left, Dr. Minkler and Secretary Winfield were half out of their chairs leaning over Mr. Saunders, who sat shaking his head emphatically and waving outstretched hands as if conjuring a barrier. From the audience came a voice no student had ever heard raised above the level of earnest enthusiasm.

"Pipe down and let him say it," Mr. Sullivan demanded. Mr. Saunders nodded agreeably and pointed an imperative finger at Minkler's and Winfield's chairs.

"How much of what we were taught will we retain?" Kevin was saying. "And for how long? A lifetime? Twenty years? How much was forgotten twenty minutes after the exam?

"Who among us knows what it means to be certain of what we know? Who knows the difference between memorizing and understanding, repetition and cognition, unquestioning absorption and independent deduction? Have twelve years of legally mandated classes taught us the value of our minds? Taught us that our minds are ours?"

"Have we been taught that thinking is not an automatic process? That it requires effort and commitment, honesty and objectivity? Have we been taught that in order to think we must *choose* to think, and that failing to choose is the same as choosing against? Have we learned that thought is a prerequisite to meaningful words and purposeful action, and that it is the quality of a thought that determines the merit of words and action?

"Or were meaning, quality, and purpose swept aside by a purposeless teacher?

"We have spent years attending mandatory classes in English. Were we shown *why* it is important to know the principles of grammar? Why there are rules of punctuation and composition? Were we shown with each new lesson, that lesson's application and relevance to our lives?

"Or were we merely told, 'This is an adjective; that's a proper noun'?

"We have spent years attending mandatory classes in history. Were we shown *why* it is important to know about the men and women who lived before us? Were we shown, with each new lesson, what role their lives and thoughts and actions might play in *our* lives?

"Or were we merely told to remember the date of the Geneva Convention and the length of the Great Wall of China?

"We have spent years attending mandatory classes in science. Were we shown *why* it is important to understand the laws of nature? Were we shown how that understanding is of value to our survival? Were we shown with each new lesson, that lesson's relationship to the world in which we live?

"Or did we merely dissect a few frogs, memorize a few theories, and watch a movie about earthquakes?

"Looking back, who among us can truthfully say: 'It was all useful and important, I understand its relevance and value to my life, I *know* it'?

"Looking back, whenever we asked a teacher *why*, did the answer make sense? Did it justify months or years of study, homework, exams? Were we answered at all?

"Or did we even ask? Perhaps we considered these years to be of such little value that we didn't mind wasting them on irrelevant subjects and forgettable assignments.

Perhaps we attended seemingly pointless classes merely because someone said we had to, that they were required of boys and girls our age, that there *was* a reason but that *we* didn't need to know it.

"Understand that if we accepted such nonsense we can be made to accept anything.

"Understand the guilt of any teacher who responded to our questions by saying, 'Because that's the rule' or 'Because that's how it's supposed to be done' or 'Because that's what's on your test' or 'Because I say so.'

"Understand that such answers were not intended to foster understanding, but obedience. That they were not the answers of a teacher, but of a dictator.

"Since learning requires a willingness to learn, some among us are, and will probably remain, unteachable. Since independent thinking is a skill the unwilling can never possess, compulsion will be all they know. But those of us willing to learn still have the means, and perhaps enough time, to discover how to think independently."

Kevin scanned countenances illumined by a descending reddening sun. He saw students with whom he had traveled along a path that led them together to this night. He saw parents and grandparents and friends, uncles and aunts and brothers and sisters. He saw curiosity, disapproval, pride, boredom, expectation, and reflection. He glanced over his shoulder and saw his father with an expression that, he thought, was not one of anger, but of tentative interest. He saw Mr. Sullivan, Mr. VanAnglin, Dana, and Rebecca, and he imagined in the empty seat beside her, Daniel.

"On this final day of the education that was to prepare you for life," he said, "this celebration of commencement into the choices of tomorrow, I offer you the words of a man who should have been your teacher.

"Teachers who know, can prove what they know. Those who cannot have nothing to teach but obedience. Reality and reason are your allies; understanding is your due.

"It is *your* mind. Do not betray it."

EPILOGUE

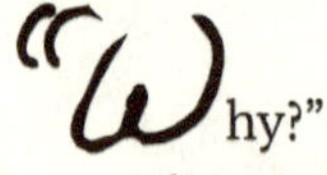

"Why?"

The teacher smiled.

"Because," he said, "it was a time when such questions may not have been answered even in school."

"Was it difficult being a student then?"

"Being a good student was difficult, but *good* as defined by that system was entirely different than *good* as defined by ours. Can you imagine attending school because the law required it? Or learning subjects of no significance to your life? Can you see yourselves studying, not for the purpose of acquiring useful knowledge, but merely to pass an exam?

"Imagine sharing class with students who don't want to learn, or who don't comprehend why they're in school."

"It must have been terrible."

"It was absurd, but few people realized it."

"Mr. Saunders," asked another student, "did you know many of those who left the country?"

"My brother relocated to Montreal," Kevin answered. "My parents talked about joining him there but never did. I had professors who lauded England and Australia; I don't know where they live now. The two I respected most have retired from teaching but are still here."

"My father's first wife went to France," volunteered a girl in the front row. "He said she couldn't bear the responsibilities of real independence. He said that the people who left did so by choice, that no one was actually forced to leave."

"That's true," Mr. Saunders agreed, "but many people believed they *were* being forced to leave because the long-established taxpayer-funded programs upon which they had come to rely—so-called free education, health care, housing, even groceries—no longer existed. Gradually, people felt 'compelled' to rely on themselves, and it wasn't long before those who couldn't began to plead and protest and violently lash out—or leave. Their logical retreat was, of course, the countries of Europe, resulting in a reversal of their forefathers' migration to what would become, for a while and then again, America."

A boy at the back of the room raised his hand.

"Allen?"

"Were they welcome in other countries?"

"Absolutely. At least for the first five or six years. Most governments wanted what was still esteemed as American ingenuity and resourcefulness. After a while, though, they began raising the cost of citizenship, requiring American immigrants to demonstrate expertise in certain fields, or the ability to invest financially. Many countries began lowering the maximum age for immigration. New Zealand, if I remember correctly, went from about fifty-three years to thirty-nine. I suspect after a while these governments realized that the new citizens they were welcoming were more of a burden than an asset, that they lacked the virtues once considered typically American."

"Mr. Saunders," asked another student, "could you tell

what was going to happen by studying history?"

"Some of us could tell what *might* happen, because even a cursory historical review indicated America's drift toward collectivism. Her thirty-second president said: 'The nation must act as a trained and loyal army willing to sacrifice for the good of a common discipline.' Thirty years later another declared: 'Ask not what your country can do for you, ask what you can do for your country.' And around the time I finished college we heard: 'Think not of yourselves, but of the planet, for it is only through global mutualism that peace and equality can be assured. Unite, be as one with your brothers and sisters, and be free!'"

A girl in the back row laughed, then said, "Sorry. But how could anyone have believed that?"

"Two centuries of incremental evasion and betrayal had cut America loose from her mooring," Mr. Saunders explained. "She was a nation adrift, guided by prevailing currents and an occasional storm. Only the rediscovery and reimplementation of the ideas that created America could true her course. And it had to start here, in education, with teachers who valued freedom and who could demonstrate the relationship between independent thinking and independent life—and with students who understood that it was their *job* to ask questions until every lesson made sense."

A bell tolled twice from a tower in the school's courtyard. Kevin wished his class a good weekend and began closing windows against the rising mid-July heat. He adjusted a thermostat on the wall by the door and arranged the material on his desk for second period.

Eight hours later he placed a stack of essays in his briefcase, readjusted the thermostat, and switched off the classroom lights. His youthful stride resonated briskly through empty corridors, sharply punctuating the silence

until he stopped in the lobby before a waist-high table arranged with textbooks and curriculum literature. He tidied
the exhibit, then took two steps back to include in his perspective the painting on the wall above it.

At the hourglass riding a turquoise sea he smiled in
salutation.

THE END

HUXLEY

The 21st Century will be the era of world controllers. The older dictators fell because they could never supply their subjects with enough bread, enough circuses, enough miracles and mysteries, nor did they possess a really effective system of mind manipulation. . . . Under a scientific dictator education will really work, with the result that most men and women will grow up to love their servitude and will never dream of revolution.

Aldous Huxley, 1894-1963
. . . Brave New World Revisited

AFTERWORD

From a Lecture at Pinkerton Academy
Derry, New Hampshire, April 1990

Today's speaker is the author of the controversial novel, Honor
Student. *The book has been spread around quickly and discretely
and has quite a following. It is about a student, much like some of
you, who is fighting for the possession and use of his mind. His
enemy? The public school he attends. Much like . . .*

*The fight is basically a lost cause at first, and what struck
me is how well it parallels today's educational system. After reading it, I, like many others, was struck by startling messages: that
nearly twelve years of school, especially the last four, were
wasted. That I was not given the education I deserved. That the
failings of schools are supported by law, and that some of the
teachers I thought were bad are, in fact, bad. That nothing will
change unless students claim what is rightfully theirs. And, also,
that nothing will change because nobody wants it to.*

*Before we all sit back in our classes and coast into college,
for once we ought to think about what has been happening. True,
this will be difficult for all to practice. There will be a chance to
ask questions at the end, hopefully, if we have the time.*

With that, I give you Mr. Michael Russell.

What Can Students Do?

About two months ago I received a telephone call from a young man who introduced himself as a senior at Pinkerton Academy. I appreciated his calling to tell me that he found a value in the book, but I appreciated even more the question he asked. When your librarian invited me to speak to you, I decided that of all the things I could say, the most relevant to you as students would be the answer to the question this young man asked.

Specifically, he wanted to know what he and his friends could do to help make noncoercive free-enterprise education a reality. Since politics and political systems are but a consequence of a nation's philosophy, I have reworded the question to address cause.

Hence it becomes for the purpose of this visit, "What can students do to encourage the furthering of the right ideas in education?"

To ask this question sincerely, the inquirer must genuinely believe that it is possible to distinguish right from wrong. He must understand that reality and morality are not unrelated parts of disconnected opinions, that the first is absolute and always the final judge of the second. And he must understand that education should be a practical means to achieving a worthwhile end.

Honor Student opens with a word that is always a question, a question that can only be answered by reference to purpose. The word is *why*, and it is the first word spoken by Kevin Saunders because it is the first word in human affairs.

Why is it the first word in human affairs? Because it seeks to identify purpose, a precondition of human affairs.

Why? Because man is the rational animal. His survival is neither instinctively automatic nor supernaturally guaranteed. It depends entirely on his use of the faculty that distinguishes him from all other species, the faculty that identifies and integrates the information received by his senses, the faculty of reason. To ask *why* is to ask: For what purpose? For what reason?

Why is the word that reduces every statement, every action, every idea to a graspable, judgeable entity. *Why* paves the way for asking how, what, who, when, and where —or entirely eliminates the need for further consideration.

From the seemingly self-evident to the profoundly technological, in the realm of human affairs *why* separates not only the gold from the ore, but the gold from the fool's gold. Asking *why* is like being a judge in a competition: the more you know about the criteria, the less frequently you need to consult the rule book. Eventually your knowledge and experience will enable you to integrate all but the most complex considerations subconsciously.

For example, take one minor noncontroversial statement. You are about to walk out of your house during a blizzard in January wearing only your slippers. Your mother says, "Sweetheart," or whatever your mother calls you, "put some clothes on."

You stop, standing naked in the open doorway as a layer of ice forms over the fishbowl in the hall.

"Why?" you ask.

To which your mother replies: A) "Because your body requires protection from the elements." B) "Because I was never allowed to do that when I was your age." C) "Because you will ruin your new slippers." D) "Because your father would disapprove." E) "Because our house has vinyl siding." F) "Because it's the law."

Obviously, it is easy to distinguish the irrelevant in an example such as this. It is easy because your conceptual ability is advanced to a level where simple concepts are dealt with automatically, subconsciously. You do not have to possess great powers of deductive reasoning to grasp the connection between subzero weather, an inappropriately clothed body, and hypothermia. You do not have to be an intellectual giant to realize that, "I was never allowed to do that" and "you'll ruin your new slippers" and "your father would disapprove" and "our house has vinyl siding" and "it's the law" are entirely beside the point—whether or not they are independently true. For you it is a simple issue with elementary connections. So simple, in fact, that irrelevant information stands out like an impertinence.

But for a two-year-old, or for someone with the conceptual maturity of a two-year-old, it is not so clear.

"Because our house has vinyl siding" would draw a blank because two-year-olds are unaware of vinyl siding. "Because it's the law" won't register either unless he has been arrested for failing to use his toddler seat while riding in a car. But "Mommy couldn't" and "you'll ruin your new slippers" and "Daddy will be mad" are, for a two-year-old, commandments to be obeyed, and in this the difference between obedience—a derivative of force and fear—and persuasion—a derivative of reason—is clearly exemplified.

When a child has developed his conceptual skills to the level where he can say, "But Mother, what difference does it make if you were never allowed?" Or, "Who cares if I ruin my new slippers in the process of freezing to death?" Or, "The fact that an action is required or prohibited by law does not make it right or wrong," he will cognitively be leaving childhood behind, and he will be on his way to thinking in *principles*.

This is an important concept. I'll refer to it several times, and if it's not clear after I've finished speaking what it means to think in principles, I encourage you to learn what it means.

Regrettably, few children develop beyond the stage of cognitive adolescence. Somewhere along the way they quit or get lost or stranded or left behind. Somewhere along the way they stop asking *why* . . . and eventually all the rest. Without rigorous conceptual training, their minds, minds that once sought answers, become passive and lame. They find themselves repeating ideas they don't understand, rebelling against conformity by joining socially unpopular groups, breeding children without a glimmer of a plan for the future, telling their children what to do without reference to reason, feeling *somehow* that *something* is missing from their lives, yet lacking the only faculty that could ever have identified itself as missing.

They trade their skateboard for a car, their paper route for a job in marketing, their Saturday-night dates for a spouse and kids, their glass of milk for a cup of coffee, their *Teen Beat* for the *Wall Street Journal*, and *Growing Pains* for *60 Minutes*. Physically, outwardly, they have left childhood behind, but having abandoned at fifteen or sixteen their potential to think in principles, cognitively they ceased to mature at fifteen or sixteen. They understand Word Perfect and Fortran, electronic ignitions and nuclear power, and most of them genuinely want to do what is "right," but the day they stopped asking *why* they traded certainty for uncertainty, independence for dependence, reason and freedom for faith and force.

In other words, whether by default or design, they traded *I know* for *they say*.

Consequently, they no longer seek answers to their questions; rather, they seek reassurance that there are no answers. Eventually their credo becomes, "Forgive me, father, for I know not what I am doing—and please don't tell me."

What are the consequences when physically mature human beings are unable to think in principles? Read the news.

> According to a Canadian-government report on the country's criminal code, women in need of food and clothing should be permitted under law to steal them. The report, commissioned by Canada's Advisory Council on the Status of Women, recommends a "statutory defense of necessity to interfere with the property rights of others in order to feed, clothe, or shelter oneself or one's children." One of the report's authors, a feminist professor of law at Dalhousie University, apparently believes that this rights nullification is justified because, she says, "being without a home is worse than having your home broken into."

> In a six-year joint venture with the Peking government, the editors of *Encyclopedia Britannica* have produced a Chinese version of the reference work. "Everybody started out from a different side of the ideological fence," said *Britannica* Vice President Frank Gibney. "Any difference of opinion," he said, "was resolved by an editorial review board of American editors and the Chinese government." When the

Chinese government claimed that the Korean War was started by South Korea, for example—despite *Britannica*'s editors knowing otherwise—the review board "settled" the dispute by declining to name who started the war. Said Mr. Gibney, "We don't feel that *Encyclopedia Britannica* has been compromised at all."

The *Visual Dictionary* is a 797-page volume containing over 3,000 "easy-to-read" illustrations instead of conceptual definitions. The American Library Association voted it the year's outstanding reference work.

According to a ruling by the federal Equal Employment Opportunity Commission, an alcoholic post-office worker who lost his job because of excessive absenteeism must be rehired with reimbursement of missed pay. The worker, Ronald Snow, filed in 1978 a complaint alleging that his alcoholism was a "handicap" against which he had been discriminated. The EEOC agreed and ordered Snow's reinstatement plus $200,000 in back pay.

As students, your job is simultaneously simple and difficult. Your job is to develop a mature ability to reason and a solid base of knowledge for the purpose of preparing for life as an adult human being. You are not here to serve your teachers. You are not here to serve your parents. You are not here to serve society.

You are not servants.

You are not here for the sake of employing your teachers or for the sake of making your parents proud or for the sake of making the world a better place in which to live. You are here solely for the purpose of preparing a foundation for *your* future.

With that in mind, reword the question. "What can *you* do to encourage the furthering of the right ideas in *your* education?"

You can act in accordance with the purpose for which you are in school. You can ask *why* until every answer is graspable and judgeable.

Why school? Why this school? Why geometry? Why economics? Why square dancing? Why Victor Hugo? Why not Shirley McClain or *Seth Speaks*? Why World War I before World War II? Why a semicolon rather than a period? Why punctuate at all?

Once you understand the purpose of a lesson, or at least have reason to believe that its purpose will be clarified as you progress, you may continue with other questions. But *why* is the cardinal question. *Why* is the key to finding value and purpose in the rest of the process, and there is only one qualification required of those who care to ask it.

The qualification is honesty. *Intellectual* honesty.

No matter how great or small your mind, you must recognize the fact that neither existence nor your consciousness can be faked, that the unreal is *unreal* and has no value. Intellectual honesty requires that under no circumstance do you ever misrepresent the truth or permit it to be misrepresented in your company, and that you never evade or fail to correct a contradiction. It requires that you mean what you say and know what you mean—and that you insist on the same from those who wish to associate with you. It requires that you practice fully and consistently every idea you accept as true, and that you neither practice nor endorse any idea you reject as false.

If there is one thing I would like you to understand after I leave here today, it is intellectual honesty.

Why, out of everything else, intellectual honesty? Because as students and human beings you have a single basic choice from which every consequence will thereafter proceed. The choice is to think or not to think, and intellectually *dis*honesty is so widespread a condition that by default it fills the void created by not thinking.

It can take many forms, including laughter, silence, mockery, etiquette, rationalization, shyness, laziness, complacency, agreement, friendship, loyalty, duty, evasion, and fear. It is intellectually dishonest, for example, to laugh at a joke you find offensive. Or to remain silent when asked by a teacher if you understand a lesson when you do not. Or to join your peers in deriding someone you respect. Or to demonstrate respect for someone you disdain.

It is intellectually dishonest to defend an idea you cannot define. Or to endorse an idea about which you have no opinion. Or to venture an opinion that is not your own. Or to fail to seek an answer on the grounds that someone else will seek it for you.

It is intellectually dishonest to unfocus your mind in an attempt to avoid responsibility for your decisions. To evade naming an act in the hope that, by refusing to acknowledge it, it will no longer exist. To give advice you do not heed. To give directions you cannot follow. To ask questions for the sake of appearing interested. To join an ideological movement for the sake of doing "something." To consider yourself right because you are in the majority, or wrong because you are in the minority. To abandon your principles when faced with the challenge of upholding them. To accept a professional position for which you are not qualified. To resent the person whose ability exceeds your own. To resent yourself for failing to achieve goals realistically beyond your ability. To give up your goals, your ideals, your life on the grounds that you live in a world that is "not of your making."

But it *is* a world of your making. Which brings me to a question I should ask of you.

At the outset of this talk I announced that its theme would be, "What can students do to encourage the furthering of the right ideas in education?" I stated that your job as students is to develop a mature ability to reason and a solid base of knowledge for the practical purpose of living life as an adult human being, and I indicated the importance of acknowledging purpose throughout every step of the process. I described intellectual honesty as the essential qualification for asking *why* and defined the term as, "meaning what you say and knowing what you mean."

I have done my best in the time available to justify the statements I have made, because I respect your right to challenge those statements. But I have not answered the question that should have occurred to you the moment I said, "What can students do to encourage the furthering of the *right* ideas in education?"

That question, which only you can know if you ever would have asked it, is: "What are the *right* ideas?"

I might have assumed that everyone here automatically knows the difference between right and wrong. I might have taken for granted the possession of an innate moral certainty, or your parents' good example, or twenty centuries of Christianity, or your willingness to blindly accept an alleged authority's moral mandate.

I might be a pragmatic politician campaigning for

your vote, or a television evangelist seeking your cash, or an inept educator striving to pacify your mind, or an Ivy League professor teaching that you haven't any, or an Adolf Hitler cashing in on the offspring of an antimind professor. I might be anyone selling anything to anybody, but the result of my effort would be dependent upon my ability to represent or misrepresent my product, and upon your ability as individuals to judge it.

Let us say for the purpose of this discussion that you *are* intellectually honest, that you understand the concept and apply it to your lives. Let us say that you have established, at least, that my subject has both purpose and potential value.

How do you judge? How do you tell right from wrong, good from evil, in the realm of ideas?

By what method do you choose freedom or coercion? Volition or chance? Principles or pragmatism? Capitalism or socialism? Reason or faith? Free speech or censorship? Individual rights or collectivism? Absolutes or compromise? Reality or mysticism? Pride or humility? Rationality or emotionalism? Purpose or chaos?

To properly understand the question of right and wrong requires a thorough study of fundamental philosophic principles—a process that could easily last many years. It is so crucial an issue, however, that at the risk of being unjustly brief I would like to indicate to you the existence of an answer, and I will hope that you choose to discover the entire answer for yourselves.

Each of us is potentially a rational being. Since *human* life requires that we act in accordance with the nature of rational beings, that we associate with one another by means of reason and persuasion rather than by force and fraud, it is our right to be treated as rational beings. But rationality, like thinking and like life, is a choice.

If we hold life to be a value and rationality to be a virtue, ideas that further the life of a rational being are good. Ideas that threaten the life of a rational being are evil. From this we can conclude that the right ideas in education are those that further the life of a rational being.

What can *we* do to encourage the furthering of the right ideas in *our* education?

We can choose to act in accordance with our nature as human beings, to think, to reason, to ask *why* and to require sensible, rational answers. We can choose to be intellectually honest and to develop an active mind as a permanent attribute. We can choose to live as rational beings, as free independent *human* beings, and we can fight without mercy or appeasement anything and everything that threatens our right to such a life.

We can choose as our standard a statement meant not for an educational system or a school or a classroom, but for free independent minds. We can apply to a lifetime of learning the words of a man who should have been, to paraphrase Kevin Saunders, *our* teacher.

> Teachers who know, can prove what they
> know. Those who cannot have nothing to
> teach but obedience. Reality and reason
> are your allies; understanding is your due.

> It is *your* mind. Do not betray it.

Thank you.

Once Upon a Time
on a Bicycle

By Michael Russell

It was not the first time he had pedaled toward a horizon thousands of miles away, but never before had there been no horizon. Under the cloud of an abandoned promise, Michael Renati relinquished every possession unable to fit in bicycle panniers with only one goal in mind: to become a stranger navigating strange lands under his own power. Headwinds and climbs, tailwinds and descents, exploration, introspection, distance, vision, resolve, saying goodbye and starting over poignantly blend with exotic-locale photography to tell the true story of a man on an all-or-nothing journey to reintegrate body and soul.

From Richard S. Wheeler, six-time Spur Award Winner and recipient of the Owen Wister Award for Lifetime Achievement:

"This is a compelling story of a long
bicycle ride, from the American Southwest
to Central America. It is an interweaving of
two journeys: one geographic and the
other, interior and ethical. As we explore
these pages we see a great adventure,
planned and executed with a realistic grasp

of the dangers—and beauties—awaiting the traveler. The gifted author's story is absorbing, perceptive, and evocative. From the seat of a touring bicycle we see country and people close-up. We sense trouble as it arrives, magic when smiles greet the rider, and comfort in villages, cities, and landscapes. This is an elegant book brimming with photographs, wisely kept to black and white, offering a visual dessert.

"*Once Upon a Time on a Bicycle* is too large to compress into genre and far more than an adventure. It is a love story."

Once Upon a Time on a Bicycle
is available in hardcover and trade-paperback editions, and as an eBook.

"**Take the hard road, if it's the right road.**"

Richard S. Wheeler, 1935-2019

Publishing, editing,
writing, bookcraft and reissue
to old-school standards of excellence.

nonesmanneslond.com

About the Author

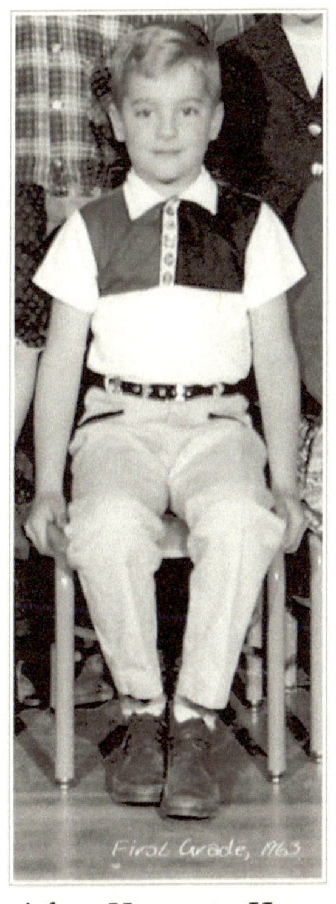

Michael Russell was inspired by an exuberant mentor in high school to pursue writing and teaching as a dual career, but uninspiring university classes were interrupted by a higher calling. His passion for innovative physical endeavors led to his winning three world cups in ballet skiing and the creation of SnowDance—a first-of-its-kind theatrical dance company on skis—and inspirited a lifelong dedication to achieving excellence in every quest. He has been a business manager, photographer, U.S. Freestyle Ski Team captain, stage actor, musician, logger, bartender, mechanic, motorcoach operator, teacher, builder, and uncompromising advocate for individual rights. He wrote *Honor Student* in 1989 and this revised edition 30 years later, *Once Upon a Time on a Bicycle* in 2018, *Winterdanse: The Misplaced Art of Snow Ballet* in 2022 (recipient of the International Skiing History Association's Ullr Award), and *The Unfounding of America: A Countdown to Too Late* in 2024. He resides off-grid in a secluded mountain valley with his wife, German shepherds, and wild-animal neighbors. He is not on social media.

www.ingramcontent.com/pod-product-compliance
Lightning Source LLC
Chambersburg PA
CBHW022357110726
47902CB00002BA/326